EA

CW00802999

2012

DEATH VALLEY SLIM

DEATH VALLEY SLIM

NELSON NYE

THORNDIKE
CHIVERS

This Large Print edition is published by Thorndike Press®, Waterville, Maine USA and by BBC Audiobooks, Ltd, Bath, England.

Published in 2004 in the U.S. by arrangement with Golden West Literary Agency.

Published in 2004 in the U.K. by arrangement with Golden West Literary Agency.

U.S. Hardcover 0-7862-6919-7 (Western)
U.K. Hardcover 1-4056-3125-2 (Chivers Large Print)
U.K. Softcover 1-4056-3126-0 (Camden Large Print)

The text of this Large Print edition is unabridged.
Other aspects of the book may vary from the original edition.

Set in 16 pt. Plantin by Minnie B. Raven.

Printed in the United States on permanent paper.

British Library Cataloguing-in-Publication Data available

Library of Congress Cataloging-in-Publication Data

Nye, Nelson C. (Nelson Coral), 1907–
    Death Valley Slim / by Nelson Nye.
      p. cm.
    ISBN 0-7862-6919-7 (lg. print : hc : alk. paper)
    1. Death Valley (Calif. and Nev.) — Fiction.   2. Gold
mines and mining — Fiction.   3. Prospecting — Fiction.
4. Large type books.   I. Title.
PS3527.Y33D44 2004
  813'.54—dc22   2004052538

I

Behind him, away back in the Panamint
Sink, the heat hung like smoke, curling and
writhing against blue-gray hills as Henry
Clay Jenkens — Pinkie, for short — cresting
a ridge on his dun-colored mule, reined in
for a breather, his glare-faded eyes suddenly
crafty with guile.

Tall, gaunt as a half-starved timber wolf,
there was something inordinately wild and
fierce in the arrested cant of that tight-
skinned face as the sharp stare quartered
the spread-out view, the head finally bob-
bing in a satisfied nod.

No one, it was said, but a fool or an
owlhoot would risk life or limb in that
burning waste where so many others had
left stripped bones to the scorching winds.
This man laughed with scorn at such fears.
Those banshee winds had sung him to
sleep for weeks on end; he'd roved Death
Valley from Dry Mountain to Ashford Mill
near the Jubilee Pass, and claimed to know
every crack and cranny of it — a brag that
wasn't too far from the truth.

Big-boned and florid, he was a sandy

haired coot in a many-patched shirt that had once been red but now was reduced through climate and wear to a blotched dingy pink, salt rimed under the arms and open down the front pretty near to the frayed twist of rope that kept up the baggy, brush-snagged pants.

His boots were Justins, bench-made to his order, sun-greened now, cracked and twisted and, like all the rest of him, blatant with run-over heels of better days. But his Chihuahua spurs, with big gleaming rowels and silver danglers, slapped back the sun bright as knife blades.

He called the dun mule Gretchen after a frail who had run him through the wringer at a time in his life when he'd been less wily and a heap more impressionable. Halted on the ridge, peering ahead again and somewhat to the east of those black towering flanks of eighty-four-hundred-foot Montezuma Peak, he might have been Hannibal or Genghis Khan, so exultant was the look of that craggy face.

Shoving back his chin-strapped steeple-crowned straw to mop some of the beaded sweat off his forehead he could not restrain a gleeful chuckle at the knowledge he'd been hugging these past sixty miles. "Yes, sir, you bald faced old skate," he told the mule, "there's a new day a-comin' an' she's just about here!" A great belly laugh shook him, and Gretchen laid back her ears as he whacked the bulging canvas sack tied with a kind of Mormon tangle behind the pommel of the cracked old saddle. He could hardly wait to see their faces!

Saddle tramp, desert rat, bum and poor risk were some of the milder tags they'd hung on him, those long-nosed, fat bellied counter-jumpers of Goldfield, and Jenkens despised every self-righteous one of them. Setting around in their lace-curtained homes, snug as church mice, with a houseful of servants ready to jump at each growl, living by grab off the fat of the land! Lying in wait like tarantulas and tax collectors to snatch all the profit from the hazardous efforts of honest men like himself, single-blanket jackass prospectors, the unsung heroes of every strike! Without men like Jenkens there'd have been no Goldfield — no Tonopahs or Bullfrogs or anything else!

But it was his turn now. The stored-up taste of his anticipated triumph was sweeter than duck eggs scrambled in honey. There was reason for much of the bitterness he nourished; he'd been right on the heels of Stimler and Marsh when those two grubstaked *hombres* had stumbled onto the float which had got Goldfield started. He had stumbled onto some himself. As a matter of fact he had made one strike and had it taken away from him, but now the shoe was on the other foot. Yet, in spite of his impatience, Henry Clay Jenkens was a cagey man. Once bit, twice shy, and he could wait a little longer to watch them eat crow.

He savored the picture, still chuckling and grinning. It did his soul good to think of those highbinders' mouths popping open as they sure as hell would when he dumped that canvas sack out in front of them. Goldfield was known as the world's richest diggings. The Alabama — it was the Mohawk now — in one recent period of 106 days had produced $5,000,000 worth of ore, and there were any number of other equally fabulous producers which numps like himself had unloaded on suckers for $300. He'd been a chump, all right — no question of that. He had learned his lesson in the school of hard knocks, but he was ready for them now. What he had in that sack was as good as the best, the kind to date time from — and *this* time Henry Clay Jenkens was going to prove himself a man to be reckoned with!

In the stimulation of this comforting reflection he chanced to glance at his shadow, seeing by the way it was bent over the ground he hadn't more than another couple hours to sundown and Goldfield was most of thirty miles still ahead. He didn't know where the day had gotten to, and swore at the mule for not getting more out of it.

A lot of gents, in his boots, would have pressed right along, too excited to relish passing time in a dry camp, but Pinkie Jenkens had wised up considerable in the three barren years since he'd made that first strike. The good news would keep. It wasn't nearly so expendable as the flesh and blood of a guy hitting Goldfield in the dark of a night with a fortune in rocks sacked back of his saddle!

In the lee of a boulder Jenkens made his camp. Not wanting to bother fooling around with grub, he hadn't fetched even the staples a man in that country generally figured to tote. So he went to bed hungry, slept five hours, caught up the mule, resaddled and went on.

Though the moon wasn't up there was plenty of starlight and the air had cooled off some, but Gretchen, who always took dry camps as a personal affront, was inclined to be sullen and found a dozen sly

11

ways to let him know her displeasure. He put up with it a while; then when wheedling and flattery failed to improve things he got off, cut a stick and let her have a good look at it. She gave a kind of resigned snort, flopped her lip a couple of times like a grouchy old woman and got reluctantly down to business.

When the moon came up at around ten o'clock the country looked more cheerful in a ghostly sort of deserted planet fashion. Its patina of blue silver draped sage and sand with a kind of unearthly beauty — not that Jenkens was connoisseur enough to notice. After all, he had more important matters to think of — like how to get the most splash out of what he was packing in that canvas sack.

This wasn't quite as simple as it might appear to be. Goldfield, though still in the boom camp phase, was a big producer of high quality ore. More than five thousand persons — nearer ten some said — were living in shacks and already it bade fair to become the most fabulous gold camp of all times. Building was going on around the clock; in some of the newest sections contractors were paying kids to hold lanterns while the carpenters worked. It had a railroad, a newspaper; brothels and saloons too numerous to count.

But, according to what he'd heard, some of the steam was beginning to leak out of things. Ore in three-figure values was still being taken from several of the mines, including the Sandstorm, the Red Top, Kendall, Jumbo and others, but a rumor was out that the Jumbo had faulted. Leasers on the Sandstorm, it was held, had been running into some strange looking ore, all of which was being dumped, and a small panic was growing if a man was to believe even a quarter of what he heard. A big strike was needed, some fresh sensation that would give the region a shot in the arm, providing ammunition the promoters could use to bolster the falling market and bring in new capital.

This was what Jenkens had in his sack, but if he aimed to move up into the mogul class he had to get all the mileage the traffic would bear. Window dressing was needed to fetch a really big splash. Ever since he'd sold out for $300, all the change he had ever got out of that town was in horse laughs and jeers. A seedy appearance might help when he emptied the sack, but even such ore — good as the best taken out of the Mohawk — was not enough in itself to lift a desert rat into back-slapping terms with the really big moguls like Wingfield, Alva D. Myers or Nixon, the banker, men who could dash off a six-figure check on the butt end of a beam or a piece of butcher paper and know it would be honored any place in the West.

That was the kind of importance Jenkens wanted. He had waited too long to get back at the scoffers, in particular Ezra P. Carltenmore, the tycoon who had fleeced him, to have any patience with anything less.

He'd been over this thing forty-eleven times now and still couldn't light on the best way to spring it. It was going to be risky no matter what approach he took. Could get him shot or strung up if he wasn't damn careful. The mildest gent in the world could go hog wild staring at the kind of stuff he had in that sample sack.

He pulled up, short of daylight, to give Gretchen another blow, but sat there chewing his lip for so long that the temperamental mule, despairing of getting fed, put her head down and disgustedly began snapping off and chomping at the handiest stems of sage.

"Hey! Cut that out!" Jenkens yelled, yanking her head up. "By grab, you can wait till *I* eat!"

He still hadn't got nothing settled in his

head. Didn't look like he was going to, either. He guessed he might as well push on. Hearing her grinding those dusty damned stems had woke his own tapeworm. He thought, A feller has to play whatever cards he gits dealt. He had the rocks, all right, no two ways about that. Now he had to expose them, and Goldfield was the place where they'd make the biggest clatter; but somebody, after that, had better watch out for the women and kids!

II

At the top of the pass he paused again for a bit, girding himself, battening hatches, trying through fluttering thoughts to find the places those buggers down yonder would pounce on. There was spots so thin the weight of a hair might open up a hole you could put a six-horse hitch through. But nothing ventured, nothing gained. Hell, Columbus took a chance! Gold and trouble was practically synonymous; all he needed was to put this to work, stir up such a rumpus he would have that bunch going round in circles. There was greed and stung pride — he would see, by grab, that there was plenty of that! There might still be a reporter or two from them big outside dailies hanging round in the hope of picking up some juicy morsel of gloom.

No smart money was going to admit the boom a bust. Too much good ore was still wheeling for the mills, too many high-graders still packing it off in the tied bottoms of their pants legs. But rumors was rumors, and folks were getting jittery. Stocks was down pretty near to where a

16

man could paper the walls with them, and Counter-jumping Ezra — one of Pinkie's pet names for that hog of a Carltenmore — had shut the Mammoth down tight, stopping all operations pending further information of that queer looking ore coming out of the Sandstorm and an alarming number of other top producers. Gad, wasn't that like him! Always playing it cagey, holding back in the hope that if the rest went into *borrasca* he might still peddle his equity at a whacking 400 per cent profit!

It was just the kind of skulduggery old Fatsides would take to. He'd got his start in this country selling java beans and sowbelly at fluctuating prices based on what he figured the traffic would bear. Two years ago, when the pass was snowed in, his beans, liberally weighted with creek-bottom gravel, had sold for as much as four dollars a pound.

He was a sharp one, all right. But supposing his drills was in that same funny ore? Or the vein had pinched out, and he had shut down his plant to keep the truth quiet? Or supposing the Mammoth, like the Jumbo, had faulted!

Jenkens' eyes began to shine. If old Stoneweight had stumbled — if he was extended enough, this could be the very handle Pinkie'd been hunting, the one loose raveling that, properly yanked, could bring all his pride and properties down into rubble with a resounding crash.

It was certainly food for some mighty straight thinking.

The road down the mountain was rocky, precarious, and flanked by the stumps of cut-over pine where trees had been whacked off for mine sets and timbers. Jenkens, though he wasn't a man to waste much thought on the ravagings of nature, found himself depressed by the sight, uncomfortably reminded of the dire possibilities inherent to bearding a tycoon of Carltenmore's caliber who had every resource of wealth and prestige, plus a conscienceless will held in leash only by the doubtful tether of what the other town bosses of Goldfield might deem winkable.

In the very nature of things these were more or less bound to hang and rattle with Ezra. It was the way of management to present a solid front to any and all not protected by the clan. Without he could get public opinion behind him it was going to be Jenkens against the whole camp.

Only a fool would fail to be worried, but

Jenkens wasn't about to back off. He'd been nursing his hate too long to quit now. They might be the brass collar dogs in these diggings but their heads was no harder than anyone's else, nor their tracks any cleaner. Let the going get tough enough they'd cut loose of Carltenmore. It plain stood to reason. On this scowling conclusion Jenkens harassed the mule until she picked up her hoofs in a kind of half run.

Didn't take her long though to drop back to normal and Pinkie, about then, became reluctantly engaged in a matter obviously calling for his sharpest attention. Coming down the final slant of the grade, rounding a shoulder that obscured the turn, he found the road blocked by a party of five — two men, one girl, a couple of kids, and three horses.

One of the men had the girl half off her horse. Both kids — a boy maybe nine and another about seven — looked frightened, and the youngest was whimpering. The feller bothering the girl showed a nasty grin. The other guy waved Jenkens round; and that was when Gretchen stopped, and Jenkens let her.

No one had to tell Jenkens what these bustards were up to. The playful sport with the leer was Pheppy Titus, flashy general super of Carltenmore's Mammoth mine and the plug-ugly with him was one of his stope bosses, Dirk Something-or-other, a big flat-faced Hunky, all bulging muscles, who'd won a heap of free drinks tying bar iron in knots with bare hands. The girl looked Mex and as such, around here, would be considered fair game by a lecher like Titus.

"G'wan — beat it!" the stope boss growled, doubling up his dukes as Titus, nastily chuckling, got the struggling girl pulled across his lap.

She was nothing to Jenkens. No quixotic notions stirred him, but his face was like stone, seeing the same roughshod arrogance and brutal indifference which so insufferably characterized everything he'd heard of Carltenmore. It was the way of their kind and suddenly, Jenkens began to see red.

"Get your paws off that girl!"

Dirk's mouth dropped open. The super was so startled, so flabbergasted by Jenkens' temerity, he let the girl get away from him. She hit the ground all spraddled out in a tangle of skirts and olive-skinned legs; and the important man's horse, crow-hopping under him, clipped her with a hoof and, by the look, must have knocked her silly. The two kids started squalling and Jenkens, swearing, jerked a gun from his shirt.

Jenkens fired, dusting off the end of Dirk What's-his-name's pants. The stope boss, clapping both hands to his seat, danced around like a Paiute who had just dropped his firewater.

Titus' eyes looked scairt.

"A fine kettle of fish," Jenkens said, motioning to where the girl had collapsed in unconscious disarray. "She's human, ain't she? Go take a look at her."

The top screw appeared to be talking up a storm but nothing came out. He wasn't getting down, either.

"Don't make me tell you again!" Jenkens snarled. Titus, visibly shaking, managed to part from his saddle. He moved like he was mounted on stilts. "Never mind her legs," Jenkens snapped. "Catch hold of her wrist and see if there's a pulse."

"She's alive," Titus mumbled, edgily bent over her. "Don't seem like anything's broken —"

"No thanks to you," Jenkens growled, looking ugly. "I oughta scatter your teeth clean to Hanner. Help her up! Brush her off! An' tell that Bohunk if he don't wanta

21

git a hand blowed loose he better stop fiddlin' around with that Arkinsas toothpick."

The girl, coming to, jerked away from the super, hauled off and belted him spang in the eye. Carltenmore's tweed-trowsered henchman let out a squawk and flopped around in a circle like a axe-cut rooster with half its feathers gone.

"That's the system," Jenkens chortled. "He's turnin' the other cheek — hit 'im again!"

This was too much for Titus. He scuttled for his mount like the hell flies was after him. But his wild gyrations and the desperate look of him put the horse's tail up and he went off down the road in a clatter of hoofbeats.

"Hoo hoo!" Jenkens jeered as Titus legged after him. Then his eyes settled cold as flint on the stope boss. "Git whackin'," he said and the Bohunk, freeing one hand from his bottom, snatched up his reins and tromped off in their dust.

For some moments the girl stared after them, rigid. Hard breathing she swung about to face Jenkens, traces of fury still bright on her cheeks. Yet brighter far was the look of her eyes, all sparkly, grateful seeming as a pup's and so filled with trust that, suddenly suspicious, he took a quick squint behind, thinking someone had slipped up on him. He didn't see anybody.

"*Gracias,*" she cried softly, "*mil gracias, señor.*"

"Well, hell," he said, "I don't want no thanks." He felt hotter than a biscuit with her staring at him that way. He peered hard at Gretchen's ears and even thought of clapping spurs to her. Females always seemed to yap the dangdest nonsense.

"I am called Dolores," she was saying, and he wished, by cripes, she would stare at something else. "My father, Elfego Ramirez, works in the mine of Señor Carltenmore. Because of this that Yanqui devil — he is bad, that one, *muy malo.* You mus' be careful . . ."

"Humph!" Jenkens snorted. "He's the one had better be careful!"

"He will not forget," she said, looking worried. Then she shook back her hair that was the color of lampblack, and said with quaint courtesy, "These are my brothers, Tomas and Alfredo."

Jenkens glanced at the kids, clinging big-eyed to their old puddingfooted horse, and nodded.

"And how are you called?" the girl asked finally, perhaps emboldened by his silence.

"¿Como se llama usted?"

Jenkens scowled. They were all alike, these women. That melting light, the butter-soft stare, the flickering lashes! He thought of Gretchen, and swore. He'd never trust another — but where was the harm? She was nothing to him. He'd never see her again. "I'm Henry Clay Jenkens," he said like a king, and threw out his chest.

"Yes," she said. "I was told you would come."

Jenkens' eyes popped. Like a crouching puma he said, *"Me!"*

"An American with red hair." She looked up at him saucily. "By the hair I should know him. Sandy and shaggy, and riding a mule."

Jenkens, feeling the spell of her, scowled. "No one knew I was coming. Who told you that?" he demanded suspiciously.

She kind of swayed and reached up, taking hold of her left arm, wincing a little, then rubbing it gingerly.

Jenkens was not to be put off. "Who said so?"

She showed a secretive smile. "A *gitana* — a — how you say? — teller of fortunes?"

"Fakes — every one of 'em!" Jenkens scoffed. "Cut the price in half an' all they'll find is hard work."

"Some of them, maybe. Not this one." She grinned. "A red-haired American," she told Jenkens dreamily. "Tall, and thin." She peered at him through the black sweep of her lashes, naively grave, and very solemnly said, "Do you feel already a little in love with me?"

"In love!" Jenkens stared aghast.

The Ramirez girl showed her dimples. She hauled in a great breath and pushed out her chest, flashing her teeth as though she looked for him to swoon.

Jenkens recognized the signs. He'd been over this road too often before. He looked at her askance, groaning under his breath. Every place was the same; she was smitten, of course — caught in the trap of his fatal charm. It was the curse of his life!

She cocked her head to one side, intently considering him. "You deny it then?"

"Look," he said patiently, "I don't even know you —"

"*No le hace.*" Dolores laughed and, as though but now remembering them, shared the grin with her brothers. "Make your manners to the American." She looked again at him, shyly, then said to the boys, "When your sister and this *caballero* are married —"

"Never!" Jenkens yelled, rearing up in his stirrups.

Both *niños* looked astonished.

"But she *said* you would marry me —"

"She!" Jenkens cursed.

Appearing fiercely affronted Tomas, the elder, whipping a knife from his sleeve, broke into a spate of furious Spanish.

"Be still!" cried his sister, her color like ashes. And she peered at the Gringo, fighting back her dismay. "You do not loff me?"

"I don't believe in that crap. Anyhow, you're too young. Besides," he said, glowering, "I wouldn't marry the best woman on earth!" And he slammed Gretchen hard with the spurs and took off.

III

Goldfield, since he'd last shaken its dust, appeared to be spreading all over the landscape. It fairly bulged at the seams. Vigor and gusto were apparent on every hand, and Jenkens began to wonder if the alleged recession was not mostly in the minds of those who talked about it. The place didn't look very sick to him. The number of saloons and allied entertainments in proportion to total growth was remarkable; but the surest harbinger of easy money, and perhaps of hidden peril, was the astonishing number of metallurgists. Seemed to be at least one to every corner. After passing the brewery and the Anaconda Mill, in one block as he worked north on Main there were six of these establishments side by side and every one of them, it looked like, crammed to the guards.

One of the signs he noticed read:

BLACKEY DAWSON, E. M.
ASSAYER & CHEMIST
Examinations and reports made on mining properties. Specialty made of Umpire and Control Assays.

Jenkens grinned wryly. No one had to tell him! A half blind camel with a gimp in one knee should be able to spot what was going on here. At least half of these buzzards, if not out and out crooks, was kissing cousins to the James boys — fences for stolen highgrade. The camp fathers weren't blind, so they had to be winking at it. He guessed they figured there was enough for everyone.

Maybe so. Another sign caught his eye.

REAL ESTATE SYNDICATE
Full Charge Taken of Property.
Money Leased on Good Security.
Business Chances Our Speciality.

For a while Jenkens studied the passing faces, what time he wasn't struggling with traffic which was occasionally so fierce it sometimes took fifteen minutes — even aboard Gretchen — to progress one block. Freighters and ore wagons banged and rattled through the heavy dust, their drivers screaming curses and snapping their whips without regard for pedestrians, fast stages adding to the bedlam with a constant and raucous chorus of shouts. Pickpockets threaded the crowded walks, competing for loot with the shell games and bunco steerers, pimps, hustlers, con men and all the rest of the two-legged scavengers who were working this lode like a convention of locusts.

By the time Jenkens had got as far north as Myers — named after Alva D. — he hardly knew whether he was coming or going. He felt light in the head and reckoned it was hunger, though he was still sufficiently in touch with his surroundings to keep one hand firmly clamped to his sample sack. In all this commotion, if a feller didn't look lively, he could have his mule stolen right out from under him.

It wasn't far now to the Goldfield Hotel, but he figured he'd better get Gretchen settled. The next street was Crook, with the Post Office off to the right, the hotel just below it and the Stock Exchange one block above. The Goldfield Club, when he reached the intersection, was scarce a stone's throw to the right, but for the moment Jenkens had no interest in brushing elbows with the moguls. To get right down to the truth of the matter he was beginning to wonder if he maybe hadn't got a bit ahead of himself. He wasn't hankering to pack any coals to Newcastle, and taking the wish for the fact would be about as stupid as attempting to bail a flooded stope with a teacup. It could knock his coup right into a cocked hat!

Reining west he pointed Gretchen toward Diall's livery. He had practically helped John get the place started and, as one of its staunchest out-of-town supporters, he hoped to get the dirt on just how things stood. They plainly weren't as bad as he'd been led to believe.

Union Hostlers Diall's place was called, and the sign read: FEED AND FUEL, HAY AND GRAIN — WHOLESALE AND RETAIL.

LIVERY. HORSES BOARDED BY DAY, WEEK OR MONTH.

It was quite a layout, and the usual loafers were squatting around whittling and testing their aim with the juice of long twist.

Jenkens saw recognition run over the gathering and as he slid off the mule old Hassayampa Smith, who hadn't done a lick of work since Marsh and Stimler had turned up their first float on a barren peak and named the camp Grandpah, said, "Look what the dang wind has blowed in now!"

And Diall, glancing up from his seat in the shade, allowed, "It's sure goin' to put an awful drain on them beer kegs," and old Smith cackled like he'd just laid a egg. One of the other local wits, folding up his knife gruffed, "He don't look snake-bit. Musta run outa whisky."

Jenkens started to inflate his chest, about to blow these ribsters plumb loose from their galluses, when some sense of proportion pushed a grin through his hackles, not an extry large specimen but one that showed anyway his heart was in the right place. "All right, you jaspers," he growled, putting the best face he could on it. "I can't help rememberin' you used to be white men, so how's about lettin' —"

"I think," Hassayampa said, *sotto voce*, "he's workin' up to a loan."

"Well," opined the stables' proprietor, "he's put over so many in the course of my experience it's hard to rest much confidence in what he says any more."

Jenkens got a little red and kind of chewed on his lip while another codger said, "Y'see that glint in his eye? Musta made a powerful strike. Sure got all the symptoms. You remember that last time? Mountain of copper, wa'n't it? Millions of tons of it!"

He slapped his thigh, and the cackles got louder. Then another whittle whanger, shoving back his hat, said, "I recollect the time he told that widder he could make a real winnin' if he could on'y git a square meal under his belt!" And Smith said, through the snickers, "Most natural fabricator I ever run up ag'in'. Told me wunst he'd counted forty Hassayampas between here an' Bannock — said if I ever meant t' git as far down as Posterity I better do like him an' latch onto a Number! Claimed he was the one put Nevada on the map, first two-legged man to ever cross Death Valley but so many dang stiffs had been doin' it since. . . . Heap of fellers don't figger he ever *did* make a strike, but I'll tell you one thing — he kin sure talk a blue streak!" And John Diall nodded. "He can certainly do that."

"Lookit the way he's swellin' up! Boys," another cried, "we better take t' the timber!"

"Set easy," Smith mooed as they started to spring up. "That ugly look on his mug is jest his natural complection. No more harm in him than you could find in a field mouse — long's you keep both han's in yer pockets. Ho ho ho!" and he laughed uproariously, throwing back his whiskery head, all the rest of them following suit.

H. C. Jenkens — or Death Valley Slim, Number 8, as he liked to be known — wasn't frothing at the mouth but he was near enough to it, flapping his hands and so dark in the face any gent who didn't know him might justifiably have suspected he was about to quit his rocker or go straight up in one mighty gout of smoke.

He was sure enough furious. But before he could get up enough tongue oil to work with, Smith declared, "Tell you the truth, he don't mean nothin' by it. He ain't onfeelin', jest fergitful is all — an' iggorant. Can't make out right from wrong no more'n a half dressed Paiute with a gallon of corn. Don't make much sense he had anything to do with settin' up this camp; but he did turn up a strike. Blowed in one day with a sackful of float which he sold Ez Carltenmore fer three hunert dollars, along with the location of what's become Mammoth Consolidated."

His listeners appeared very properly impressed. But when Jenkens, somewhat mollified, seemed about to give way to a burst of oratory, Hassayampa Smith waggled a cautioning finger. "He's one o' them things a man's got t' live with, like the small pox an' fever an' the Saint Vitus dance. I dislike bein' harsh but there's some things you jest got t' face up to, an' the truth is that Slim here's a mighty pore risk. All a feller'd have, if you took him to court, is mebbe a lien on somethin' already so plastered a Chinese lawyer couldn't git it enough unraveled to —"

Jenkens let out a yell that set half the nags in Diall's stable to pitching. Head down, arms flailing, he went for Smith with blood in his eye, but the old coot, nimbly jumping aside, stuck out a foot and sent him crashing into a wall. Before Jenkens could extricate himself from that predicament Smith went swarming up a ladder into the loft.

The rest of them, backing off, had mostly got shaken loose of their grins and now stood watching him a little askance. A guy crazy as Slim might make out to do anything. It looked best to give him plenty of room.

Jenkens, standing there appearing sort of dazed, didn't seem near as funny as he had. There was a kind of baffled look about the roving of his eyes that may have made two or three of them just a little ashamed, baiting a feller that didn't have all his marbles. A couple of these inconspicuously left. The rest closed ranks as Slim, rubbing his head, passed a hardening glance over that sea of still faces.

"That the way you feel?" he said to John Diall.

"I don't want no trouble, Slim."

"How much of a bill do you have again' me?"

"That's all right."

"You ever grubstake me?"

Diall shook his head.

"You ever sell me anything on tick?"

When the man didn't at once reply, Jenkens said, "I got this mule from you. Is she paid for or ain't she?"

The man was regarding him carefully, a thoughtful look flickering back of his stare. "I guess we're square on that mule," he finally said.

"How about you?" Jenkens demanded of another. "You've kept her in plates — how much *you* got comin'?"

The blacksmith sighed. Then, running his look across the sack tied back of Gretchen's saddle, he gruffly said, "You don't owe me a cent."

"Then have a drink on me," Jenkens insufferably cried. He flung his last two-bit piece into the dust, snorting as the hoof-shaper jumped to snatch it up.

With his lip curled back, Slim's contemptuous glance encountered the rabbity eyes of Phineas Misch who ran an outfitter's supply house and grocery on Main and had likewise felt the touch for which Jenkens' enemies had made him famous.

"Well," Jenkens sneered, "if you got anythin' coming now's the time to open your bazoo."

Misch backed away but stopped at the door. "I know when I'm well off," he growled, "but there's a cure fer you an' —"

"If you're referrin'," Slim said loftily, "to the handout you put up two years ago *I* never ast for it, and a ten-dollar bill would've covered the works. Who you think you're takin' in, anyhow?"

The man scraped up a frozen smile. "Ten dollars or a hunert, I know the law; an' I guess that goes fer Mr. Carltenmore, too! A grubstaker in this state's entitled to *half.* When you locate your find ol' Ezra P will come down on you like the top of a mountain!"

Jenkens doubled his fists, and the storekeeper fled.

Still kind of red in the face but too filled with his intentions to let that pipsqueak's spleen put him long off his game, Slim got his canvas sack off the mule, hefted it onto a shoulder, and magnanimously declaimed, "Never let it be said that Henry Clay Jenkens was too thin-skinned to remember his friends. I'll tell you, boys, I ain't et in two days — I'm so dadburned weak I can scarcely stand up, but if you wanta step over to the Northern for a minute the drinks is on me, an' —"

He broke off, glaring at their skeptical grins. Not a man had got up, not a loafer had stirred.

"Well, for Pete's sake," he blared, "don't tell me you're so proud you're passin' up free drinks!"

"Free?" Old Smith cackled, showing his toothless gums. "You'll hev t' do better'n that, won't he, boys?" There was a chorus of growls at Jenkens' darkening looks. "You're a sharp lad, Slim, but you've worked that vein too close. We're onto your dodges. You ain't stickin' me fer no round of free drinks."

"Why, dang your eyes I'm *payin'* — can't you hear?"

"Not with my money you ain't!" Smith jeered from his perch in the loft. And somebody else muttered, "On'y thing a man kin look to git from you is bills!"

Jenkens, glowering, slapped the sack on his shoulder. "I got enough right here to keep you in chawin' for the rest of your lives." But it was plain they'd heard about Greeks bearing gifts: and one of them, staring hatefully said, "Who'd you rob this time?"

"All right, you dumb wallopers!" Singling out Diall, Jenkens arrogantly demanded, "You gonna take care of this mare mule of mine?"

"I've quit doing business on credit," Diall said. "From here out it's cash on the barrelhead."

"Then stick out your mit," Jenkens angrily said. And when, a bit uneasily, the liverykeeper did, Slim, rummaging a rock from his pocket, slapped it into it. "I guess you're not above acceptin' plain gold. Give her nothin' but the best an' don't look for me till you see me."

Diall's jaw, when he peered into his hand, appeared to drop about a foot. His eyes stuck out like two knots on a stick. "What the heck is it?" clamored the others, crowding around; and Hassayampa scrambling down the ladder, said, "Some kind of a trick — you kin bet on that."

The breath that finally soughed from Diall's blanched cheeks clawed its way through his whiskers in a kind of beat groan. He peered around with a glazed stare. "Boys," he said like it was dredged from his bootstraps, "this doggone rock's purty near *solid gold!*"

IV

Still seeing red and fuming under his breath Jenkens walked back to Main, slammed into the Mohawk Saloon and gloweringly tramped through the crowd in the bar; no one gave him so much as a tumble, not even the smile they might have thrown to a dog. Finding a vacant table in the establishment's restaurant he put down his sack and flopped into a chair, ordering a meal big enough to feed three.

While he was bitterly rehashing the reception given him by that bunch at the Hostlers the waitress came back with a lumbering ape whose out-of-shape nose and unbending stare had all the earmarks of belonging to a bouncer. He had the finesse of one, too. Leaning across the table on the flats of his hands he said without beating around any bushes, "You make a habit of orderin' meals big as this?"

Slim's blood began to boil. "An' what if I do?"

"You got the money to pay for it?"

Jenkens' eyes began to glint. "You take that tone to every gent that comes in?"

"Just answer the question. Can you pay for it or can't you?"

Not entirely sure he could handle this walloper, and in no mood to be given the bum's rush, Slim took refuge in the kind of rhetoric Carltenmore employed, demanding as though affronted, "Do you know who I am?"

"The only thing I want to know is *can you pay fer it?*"

Taking his fists off the table, shrugging out of his coat, the guy tossed it to the hasher and began rolling up his sleeves. Jenkens scowled and, with a snort, sent the sack at his feet flying into the aisle. "Before you get yourself tied into a knot mebbe you better have a look at them samples!"

After scowling a moment the feller picked up the sack, fished out a piece of ore and held it up to the light. He looked again at Jenkens unreadably, gave the girl a nod and, still hefting the rock, took back his coat and went poker-faced off without opening his mouth.

Jenkens left the sack where it was on the table.

It was a good meal they brought him. He had a hard time, however, getting out of his mouth the taste put into it by the kind of people a man had to deal with in this country any more. It was enough to cramp rats! But the feller he wanted most of all to get back at was that fat tub of lard who had stolen his good prospect, made him look like a fool and then, adding insult to injury, had patronizingly and publicly announced that he was staking Slim to go out and hunt for another. True, Jenkens had belligerently told the old grasper where to go with his grubstake, but that hadn't lifted the curse and now Slim was nursing a disquieting suspicion that Carltenmore had gone out and bought up his bills.

One thing was for sure — he hadn't done it personally. The mine he'd developed out of Slim's $300 hole in the ground had made him a power to be reckoned with, even here in the most fabulous camp of all times which Bob Edgren, the noted sports columnist, had described as "a town entirely surrounded by men with from one to one thousand mining claims each." Ezra P. couldn't afford to besmirch his newly acquired big mogul status by being hooked up to such a flimflam as that. But he could do it under cover, working through agents.

There were plenty of masterless men tramping round, grifters and bravos who, so long as the pay proved sufficiently attractive, would turn their hands to just about anything. Thugs and footpads came a dollar the dozen; it took a few cents more to get a man's throat cut, but if you crossed enough palms anything a man wanted could be bought here in Goldfield where it frequently was remarked the crooks were so thick they needed identification tags to keep from selling their worthless wares to each other.

Slim noticed one thing. Though the room was pretty well filled, a good many of these chairs were being held down by shills and other fancy Dans who were spending "house" money to keep up the front. The paying customers were scattered pretty thin.

He was on his fourth cup of java and halfway through his second cut of pie when he became aware of being lengthily inspected. Looking up he found a brace of men stopped by his table. Both were quietly dressed. The one in the derby — he had a fat cigar between the clamp of his teeth and stood flicking his coat lapel, said, pleasantly enough, "If you don't mind, Mr. Jenkens, we'd like a word with you."

"God's ozone is free. Help yourself," Slim growled.

The non-smoker said as they slid into

the chairs, "Thought you was smarter than that."

Jenkens said, "What's that supposed to mean?"

"You denyin' you paid for this grub with pyrites?"

Slim's eyes opened wide. Pyrites was one of the sulphides, a common mineral, brass-yellow in color and of a brilliant metallic luster, but not anything a seasoned prospector like Jenkens would be apt to mistake for the real McCoy. Fool's gold it was called; he named it loudly and snorted. Then his stare winnowed down to glittering slits, and he came out of his chair with a gun in his fist.

The guy in the derby, the one with the cigar, showed his teeth in a grin. "Relax," he said, chuckling. "That Larry! He's just got to have his little joke."

"Mebbe you oughta tell him," Jenkens said over the gun, "a rusty like that can git a man damn quick killed."

A kind of freeze crawled over their faces, and the Larry gent's mug in the lengthening silence went about three shades paler. The Adam's apple bobbed in his neck like a fish cork. The quiet spread around them, lapping nearby tables; and the other guy took the cigar from his face and, scraping his chair closer, sort of hunching his shoulders, out of the side of his mouth said, "We're attractin' attention."

"We'll attract a lot more if this dewclaw slips."

Both men began to sweat. The head waiter was standing where he could see Jenkens' pistol. He stood wringing his hands and looked pretty upset but made no move to come any nearer. There was quite a bunch of folks watching. The gent in the derby eyed the tip of his cigar. "I had hoped we could do a little business with you. It was suggested —"

"By the L. M. Sullivan Trust I bet!"

The guy under the derby looked a bit taken aback, then his smile reappeared and he went into his patter with all the glib skill of the professional tipster. "You'd be absolutely right. Someone did approach the Trust, but of course a financial institution —"

"You can save your breath. You think I'm feeble in the head, or somethin'?" Jenkens skewered him with a scathing glance. "I been around these parts a fortnight or two. I know all I need to know about that bucket shop —"

"Now see here —"

"I spotted you, Rice, soon's you come outa that hole in the woodwork. Just git this straight —" and Jenkens looked the cigar-smoker hard in the eye, "stay outa my hair — an' I mean *all the way out,* or that fancy Sullivan front you've put up is gonna come down round your gaiters like a sack of beef stew!"

The guy's cheeks, swelling, grew darkly dismal. His mouth turned mean. Hate writhed in his stare, but it was plain Slim had him where the hair was short. This was George Graham Rice who, though not at this time generally regarded as such, was to be subsequently unmasked as the infamous swindler who almost wrecked Wall Street. He was the guiding genius behind the Sullivan Trust which, amid much fanfare, had opened its gilded doors in Goldfield, smugly claiming to employ one hundred clerks and stenographers to handle its farflung business which ultimately was discovered to be the peddling of fraudulent stocks.

How Jenkens got onto him has never reasonably been explained. Maybe it was just bluff or perhaps, more shrewd than has generally been conceded, behind Rice's suave veneer Slim glimpsed a kindred soul. Whatever the truth — and it's been argued aplenty, Rice did not crowd his luck any further. With a shrug he pushed back, his look as flat as fried flounder. "I was only trying to help," he sighed.

"Just keep outa my way." Slim shoved up with a snort. Twirling his sixgun in the road agent's spin, you saw the shine of it one minute, the next it was gone. Then he grinned like a wolf, grabbed up his sack and strode from the room.

V

Through the wind and dust came a flutter of paper as Jenkens stepped from Denny Sullivan's doors. The battered straw sombrero that was cinched to his chin bucked and flapped as he wildly dived for the newsprint, finally managing to get a boot squarely on it. After the zephyr streaked past Slim picked up his prize. Wasn't much of it left, just the tattered back page of yesterday's *News*, and not a thing on it that suggested bad times. He guessed they weren't likely to print anything which might tend to hurt business. He pitched it away, swearing under his breath.

It wasn't that he wished hard luck on anyone — always excepting, of course, that danged Ezra P! But he was smart enough to know the state of Goldfield's economy could make a heap of difference to the deal he had in mind. Timing, in financial circles, was the essence, the abracadabra that could make or break.

Jenkens didn't pretend to understand the inner workings. But there appeared to be, in this sort of thing, a kind of secret rhythm or hair-spring balance, too mixed-up and high-flown for any plain-dealing single-blanket jackass prospector to corral or even catch a fair grab at. What Slim needed if he was to get any real play out of his bear trap was to jump the market on a downhill swing.

He was standing right here at the main intersection, the busiest crossroads of the camp's turbulent life, the flossiest four corners of the town's principal arteries, crowds all around him and the streets jammed, too. Behind him was the doors of the Mohawk. Over there was the Palace. Across from it the Hermitage, and on the fourth corner Tex Rickard's Northern Saloon and Gambling House. Two blocks away — one block east and one more north — was the Stock Exchange, and he was seriously considering going up there for a look. Only trouble with that was it might put ideas in them bigwigs' heads. One piece of his ore was already in circulation, the chunk he had put up to pay for that meal, and the way rumors traveled. . . .

Jenkens swore again. Looked like he was committed! That chunk had been worth around two hundred dollars — and he hadn't even waited to get back his change!

He sighed and groaned and cursed some more. He didn't know what to do hardly. He felt like a man with a bear by the tail. Mauled if he did and clawed if he didn't. He thought of Rice again. Him and his loud-mouthed stooge Shanghai Larry must be sure enough scraping the bottom of the barrel if they'd got down to working desert rats for their pickings.

"Well, here goes nothin'," he growled with a grimace and, toting his sack, stepped right into the turmoil and racket of surreys and beer drays, freighters, buckboards, spring wagons, horsebackers and even a splatter of half-drunk Injuns. Such a storm of invective a man never heard as brake blocks screeched and red-faced, perspiring, fist-shaking drivers shouted abuse in a dozen languages.

Having gained the far walk Slim, not lingering to take in the damage, jumped like a rabbit through the slap of Rickard's batwings. The place was jammed pretty near bad as the street. Men were packed three deep along the sixty-foot bar and not one of the twelve sweating aprons but what was using both hands. No one turned or looked up, and it gave Slim a glimpse of something he sure didn't very much care for the looks of. "Whew!" he said, shaking, not convinced even yet he still had all his parts.

Rickard's Northern was the most celebrated and consistently patronized of all the thirst-quenching places in the town, and has been generally rated the most successful and high voltage gambling resort the West ever knew. There were fourteen games, and not a one of them was idle — three crap tables, three roulette wheels, an equal number of faro layouts and five blackjack setups. Three shifts of bartenders worked around the clock and it was common knowledge they emptied six barrels of whisky, in addition to great quantities of wine, gin and beer, every day. Completely ignored, Jenkens had not felt so all-fired alone clean out in the middle, by grab, of Death Valley!

It was a sobering thought, and one that pretty near made his big coup appear about as important and likely as a .22 cartridge in a eight-gauge gun.

Then a man, stepping up and taking hold of his arm, said, "Ain't your name Jenkens?"

He was a beat-up looking sort of jigger with a dark and hungry hound-dog face in a store-bought suit with shiny elbows and wrinkled enough to have been slept in a week. A brown dilapidated derby was precariously cocked above the puffier of two saddlebagged eyes, and the blue-black jowls could have done with a scraping. Despite the corrosions of world-weariness and cynicism so markedly apparent in this unkempt face there was something in the sardonic look of it which made the wily prospector pause. "Yeah?" he said.

"The one they call Death Valley Slim?"

"That's me," Jenkens growled. "Number Eight — what about it?"

"Scoop Featherstone here." The guy pushed out a hand which, when Slim ignored it, Featherstone flexed, showing the edge of a crooked grin. "If you've time to wet a whistle I'll be glad to stand the drinks."

"Ain't you one of them newspaper fellers?"

"Temporarily unemployed," the man smiled, and Jenkens flashed him a cagey stare. "Howcome you didn't clear out with the rest of 'em?"

Featherstone laughed a bit ruefully. "That's why I'm out of a job," he sighed; then, sobering, said, "Just call it a hunch. You care for that drink?"

"Why not?" Slim said, skinning the lips back off his big teeth.

There was another gazabo at Featherstone's table, gray as a timber wolf and all
togged out in Sunday collar and hames.
"Slim, meet Sam Reilly. Sam was a broker
till the suckers took fright and hocked all
their stocks for a ride out of town."

Jenkens' eyes flashed but he was careful,
in sitting, to stay enough away from the
table to lower his handicap in the event
there should be any sudden scramble for
guns.

Reilly said without hope, "If you happen
to have any Jumbo shares you might like to
get rid of I could prob'ly find some half-
awake numbskull we could talk into taking
them off your hands."

"Don't you ever quit trying?" Featherstone joked. Then he said, eying Slim,
"Might's well face it. We got all the mak-
ings of a damn good bust."

"Why, this camp," Jenkens hooted, "ain't
hardly yet scratched the pinfeathers off!"

"I can see you're an optimist," the reporter said sourly, and ticked off his rea-
sons on three held-up fingers. "The Jumbo
has faulted; there's no doubt about it.
There's that queer looking rock the Sandstorm's been dumping. Now the Mammoth's shut down. These are facts. You
can't blink them."

"Mebbeso," Slim conceded, "but they're taking better ore out of the Combination, the Mohawk, the January an' Red Top than ever — an' a heap more of it. No camp's goin' bust on them kinda profits."

"I don't know how much is profit," Featherstone growled. "There's a lot of highgrading. It could be pretty ruinous. Used to carry it off in their lunch baskets. I'm told that now, in the Florence, the miners are all wearing outsized pants and stuffing both legs."

Jenkens scoffed. "Them moguls may not like it," he said, "but —" and he stopped right there, looking cagey again.

Featherstone said, "Big Three's been augering every night this week, ticker tapes whirrin' like a nest of diamondbacks. That road the Tonopah and Tidewater people was building on paper is being given another look."

"You put me in mind of Al Hart," Jenkens grumbled. "He was in with Alva Myers on the Combination claims; never could believe they'd ever amount to anything — let a Tonopah faro dealer buy him out for a few hundred bucks. Ole Elliott came in an' traded the gambler out of Hart's shares for a measly ring an' the next month sold out for seventy-five thousand, joinin' Hart an' Graham at cussin' their luck when the new pardners begun shippin' carload after carload of some of the fanciest dang rock they'd ever popped eyes at. One forty-eight ton carload fetched a smelter check for five hundred an' seventy-four thousand nine hundred and sixty-eight dollars an' thirty-nine cents!"

"That's talking!" Reilly chortled, clapping Slim on the shoulder. "That's what the investors like to hear. What we need is more gents like you — guys with a little faith an' vision!" Then he lowered his tone enough to sound confidential. "When the market sags the smart money sings."

Jenkens' stare turned thoughtful. Then the waiter came up with a rag over his arm. "Make mine Gold Nugget beer," Slim said. Reilly, scratching his belly, put in a bid for Old Crow with branch water and Featherstone signified he'd try the same; and all this while his eyes stayed on Slim.

The waiter hurried off. Slim said, "You must of had your good ear to the ground," and grinned at the newshound knowingly. "If you believed that crap you'd of gone with the rest."

"All right," Scoop said. "I'm playing it by ear. What this camp needs is a shot in the arm. You look like the one I'm going to have to do business with."

Jenkens batted his eyes. "How's that?" he piped, putting up a hand and cupping his ear like a guy in his dotage. "You mind ridin' over that trail again?"

Featherstone grinned. "Might even be a pleasure." And Reilly, hunching closer, said, "What kind of stuff you got in that poke, boy? Good as that chunk you give old Friedface?"

Jenkens looked like a greenhorn nursing four aces. "Friedface?"

"Guy in the boiled bib — that Mohawk bouncer."

"Oh, *him!* That was a float. Picked it up over around Lone Pine."

"Ha, ha!" Reilly laughed, poking Scoop in the ribs. "Just float, eh? When you're ready to capitalize, let me know. I'll get out a stock issue —"

"Boys, that's the Gawd's awful truth. I combed them ledges for nigh onto a week an' never found another piece. Might of gone to around five thousan' a ton," he admitted, covering his mouth with a hand, "but it wasn't in a class with that carload I mentioned."

Reilly laughed some more. "Hardly better'n that stuff they been throwin' away, eh? Slim, how'd you like to own a block of Sandstorm stock?"

Jenkens grinned, too, and picked up his beer. "Tell you what I'll do," Reilly said. "I'll give you two hundred shares for what you've got in that sack. Free and clear."

"Can't hear you," Slim chuckled, setting down his empty glass. "Tell you one thing, though. I wouldn't throw it away."

Reilly's glance showed a sharpening interest. Then he said, staring reflectively into his drink, "I was sitting right there, not three tables off, when you dug out that nugget. That feller turned white as a bed sheet. His eyes damn near come out of his head! If this was handled right . . ."

"Drink up," Scoop said, "and we'll have another round."

Slim never even noticed he had a full glass again. He poured it down, scared up a burp. "Great stuff — don't care if I do."

The waiter came and set a fresh glass at his elbow. Reilly said, "How you fixed for cash?" and Jenkens shrugged. The reporter groused. "There's a scoop here somewheres if I could just get my hooks in it."

Ten beers later Jenkens confidentially said, "If it was worth my while I could prob'ly scrape up a few headlines fer you," and sat back looking happy as a guy who had them all.

Featherstone ran a rumpling hand through his hair. "Heads," he scowled, "is for them drones at the office. What *I* gotta have is a goddamn *story!* The goddamnder," he belched, "the better!"

Jenkens, blinking owlishly, said, "I c'ld take care of that, too!" and peered around with the sort of belligerence that dared anyone to lift a skeptical eye. Reilly, busily wrestling papers from a pocket, couldn't help feeling this was moving along some slicker than slobbers, but he didn't back off. Shooting fish in a barrel was an old game with him. Who but a chump would waste pity on a sucker? And he sorted his gaily colored papers out in piles.

Jenkens looked to have difficulty fetching the reporter into focus but his tongue was sure oiled right up to the nines. "When a gent gits the chanct," he was declaiming, "t' kick the skids right out from under one of the biggest, highbindin'est nobobs in this camp a few extry lumps don't make no difference a-tall — not a pukin' bit, if you git what I mean? You stick with me, chum, an' I'll git you a story that'll — But you'll have t' make it worth my while, understand?"

Featherstone said, "How much will it cost me?"

"How much you got?"

Scoop scratched his chest. "Fifty bucks?"

Jenkens glared like a grampus. "Five hundred! I could make as big a splash with a pea as fifty bucks!" And he reared onto his feet, reaching out for his sack.

Featherstone growled. He looked pretty disgusted. "What's the matter with using some of the rocks in that bag?"

"Never you mind what's in that bag," Jenkens muttered. "You heard my price. Take it or leave it." He picked up his sack.

"And where would I get any five hundred smackers?"

Slim's eyes turned cunning. "You can git it. Wire your paper — ain't nothin' you newshounds won't do fer a story."

Featherstone's fingers drummed a while on the table. "You don't know what those editors are like back East. Can't you give me a hint?"

"E.P.C. An' the E stands for Ezra." Jenkens relished the start the newsman couldn't quite hide.

"Well," Scoop grumbled, thinking it over, "what about him?"

Slim, shouldering his sack, appeared about to head for the door. Featherstone threw up his hands. "All right. You'll get your money."

"Before supper," Jenkens grinned, "an' I'll want it in gold twenties — somethin' a man can jingle in his pockets."

The reporter looked pained but said he'd remember. "Better have another drink," Reilly urged, looking up. "Seal the deal."

Slim dropped into the chair again. He put the sack in his lap. Reilly played with his papers. Featherstone dug a stenographer's shorthand book from one of his coat pockets and started sharpening a pencil. "Let's get this going —"

"Only thing I promised was to git you a story."

"So I'm ready."

"You ain't gettin' a thing till I git hold of that jingle. What do you take me for — a dang fool!"

"You could at least," Reilly said, "give us a look at those rocks."

Slim thought about that. He took a look around the room, untied the neck of his sack and leaned forward. "I'll trade you a chunk fer two hundred dollars."

Reilly looked to see if Slim was pulling his leg. "Well, okay," he gruffed finally. "We'll have to go over to —"

"What's the matter with right here?"

"You want it in gold?"

Slim tied his sack and got up. "Let's go."

"Now just a damned minute!" Scoop growled, looking sore. "If I'm kicking in five hundred —"

"Here!" Slim cried, digging a piece out of his poke. "An' if you figure on gettin' the rest of this yarn fetch along that jingle an' look me up before supper. I'll be in the best suite at the Esmeralda Hotel."

VI

If he was pied-eyed and maybe not the smartest looking dude this side of Las Vegas, kind of tacking along with seven sheets in the wind, he felt anyway as chipper as a boxful of hoppers, wallowing into the Esmeralda leaking double eagles all over the carpet.

You talk about attention! Listen — he had it! Bellboys and porters scrambling around like monkeys in a peanut heaven. Even the star boarders, who had settled their paunches in the wing chairs and sofas, broke off their windies for a moment, and a couple weren't above attempting to trap a little twinkler 'neath the surreptitious lowering of a high-topped button shoe. Even had there been no prospect of gain he would still have got a bang just out of looking at their faces.

The hired help fetched about half his dandies back, but Slim waved them away with a grin and a wink. The high and mighty desk man, blowing like he'd run half a mile and completely ignoring the new guest's unsavory appearance and lack of luggage, swung the book about with an ingratiating smile. "Welcome to the Hotel Esmeralda — running hot and cold water, baths, electricity and a genteel decorum. Will you be with us long, Mister . . . er . . . ah?"

"Jenkens," Slim said. "Henry Clay Jenkens, Three," and, with all the curlicues of copperplate, scrawled it clear across the page. "Can't say, off hand." The manager backed off a bit to get out of the mule stink and Slim, pinning him with a glittering eye, demanded to be shown the best suite in the house.

Although obviously used to accomodating himself to the peaks and plateaus of the prospecting trade where anybody might blossom into a nabob, the manager uncomfortably, though with pardonable caution, treated himself to a second look at Jenkens. He was not reassured, but the memory of all those twinkling double eagles and Slim's subsequent largess struck a heavy balance in the desert rat's favor. The bell captain was summoned. "Show Mr. Jenkens the Buckingham Suite."

"Right this way, sir." With the deference accorded only the most opulent, the lackey in the monkey suit wafted Slim over to the elevators, got him aboard and whisked him up to the fourth floor. Down the long

deeply carpeted corridor he led, rattled a
key in a lock and threw open a door.
"Three rooms," he observed, "all done in
Old English — flossiest joint in the
dump." He grinned.

Slim peered about in considerable awe.
Then, remembering the audience, sniffed a
couple times and said he reckoned it
would do.

"Very good, sir. And would there be anything else?"

Slim dug out another of his gold pieces,
but just as he seemed about to cross the
guy's palm he paused, staring fishily, to
say, "Like what?"

"Drinks, sir?"

"Well," Jenkens said, "you might fetch
up a keg of Gold Nugget beer an' — Say!
How does that fan work?"

"Allow me, sir."

He got the thing started and dragged a
glance across the bed which looked big
enough, Slim thought to anyways sleep
five. "The bath, sir, is in here." The guy
took his monkey suit through an open
arch, and directly Slim heard the drop and
splash of running water. The feller came
back. "I've taken the liberty, sir —"

"I got ears," Jenkens growled. "You fixin'
t' scrub me, too?"

"Ha ha!" The guy put a grin across his teeth, then considered Slim slanchways. "Could I — ah — make a suggestion, sir?"

"What is it?"

"You have the look of a man's kind of man. I was just thinking sir, if you should happen to feel like — ah — having a little company," he winked, "I could —"

"If you're pimpin' fer some female," Jenkens growled, "you better take off while you're still in one piece. An' another thing, bozo! I'm pretty free-fingered when it comes to the tips, but don't have your hand out every time I turn round. When I'm ready I'll take care of you — savvy?"

The guy said, red-faced, "Of course, sir. Of course!" and got himself into the hall in a hurry.

"Some crust!" Jenkens snarled, turning the key in the lock. That was all they could think of, getting hold of your money. He didn't mind shelling out if there was good to be got from it, but with a feller like that you'd just be throwing it away.

He hiked into the bathroom and shut off the water. Then he hauled off his clothes and got into the tub. He relished the thought of a nap in that huge ocean of feathers.

It took him a while to work out a system of alarms and precautions which in the long run promised some relief to the mirrors. When he awoke suddenly and saw that galoot coming for him with them bugged-out eyes and a fist driving beltward he done what any other coot with good sense would — half emptied his shooter before he caught on. He was some put out to be taken in like that by his own face, so while his dander was up he knocked the rest of the glass. Quite a hubbub got loose in the hall outside, shouts of men and females screaming, slamming doors and all the rest of it till you'd have thought, by grab, there'd been a massacree or something! Time the hotel dick and a brace of his monkey-suited understrappers fought through the jam and with a passkey got the door flung open Slim, reloaded, was ready for all comers. The big bugger's eyes nearly rolled off his cheekbones when he saw all that glass scattered over the wickiup. Seemed like he was going to choke in his tracks; then, patchy cheeks still swollen, he took another look, flapped his arms and stomped out, herding his henchmen and the goggling crowd with him.

It cost Slim twelve double eagles, and he

had to do some pretty tall talking to keep his pistol out of the hotel safe. By this time he'd had his seance with Scoop Featherstone, so could bail himself out, but it left a few scars on his public image.

He sulked in the bar for a spell after that, still hitting the beer and feeling hard used. The weight of what was left of what was still in his pockets finally decided Slim to return to the Northern, but there he was just another crazy desert rat that nobody seemed to have any time for. These were mostly new faces, and the few gents he saw who had reason to recall Slim passed him off with a nod, showing little inclination to improve their acquaintance.

Jenkens, cursing, quit the place in a huff.

But outside the batwings he ran into Sam Reilly. Sam grabbed and danced him around, whooping and chortling, friendly as a blood brother. "Beginnin' to get around some," he said through his chuckles. "Ain't caught up yet with the man on the street, but just give it time. You might even have to hide out for a bit when some of those jaspers you've run up a bill with — Hell, you're going places, boy! That piece you sold me'll run forty thousand to the ton!"

Slim perked up some and threw out his chest.

Reilly thumped him. "This ought to call for some kind of celebration," he said sizing him up while he pummeled and pounded. "Appears to me you're headed straight for Nob Hill. I'll say this, I sure hope when your boots gets as big as George Wingfield's and Ezra's you'll still count me on the hand with your friends."

And Slim said, half crying, "Old chum, don't you *know* it?"

It was full dark now, though the town threw out such a blaze of lights a man would hardly notice without he looked up to see. Everywhere a man turned there were people, some places so crammed they spilled out into the streets — and all of them wagging their jaws every-which-way. Pretty exciting, Slim thought. Never see nothing like it; but in a different kind of way he found it rather appalling. So when Reilly suggested they look in for a spell at the Goldfield Club he'd have settled for anywhere that held out a hope of less stir and more quiet.

Seemed a considerable number of people there, too — mining tycoons with a sprinkling of supers and a shoulder-locked clot of high-booted engineers. There was even, rubbing elbows at the far end of the bar, a couple of cow-raisers in big hats, their short sides sagging to the weight of belted pistols.

Had Slim been in a more noticing shape he'd have seen the sly way Reilly's eyes batted round, and maybe wondered a little how they'd stayed all night so quick at that place. As it was he let himself be taken in tow like a orphan calf, never giving a cuss whether school kept or not — never thinking, in fact, no more than a cheek strap, content to waller along in a beery haze wherever old Sam seemed to feel they had to go.

After finally taking care of one of the more pressing calls of nature, he figured he'd better be watching himself or he might turn out to be as polluted as he looked. Shoving a finger down his throat, and heaving three or four times, he felt a little more up to making a night of it. Pushing through a door he found himself, with no sign of Reilly, back in the blue haze of the Goldfield Club's bar. Strangely enough, the first face he made out coming round from a bar stool was that of Scoop Featherstone.

"Gents," the reporter said, walling his stare about and lifting his voice above the drone of the gab, "we have with us tonight one of three who lay claim to having founded this camp." And he thumped the bar with his beer mug by way of making sure he had their fullest attention. When all heads came around he waved his free hand at Jenkens. "The man, moreover, who may yet save our tottering temples of iniquity; who, through his own unflagging single-handed efforts, may be destined to become the mightiest mogul of this town. I give you: Death Valley Slim — Number Eight."

The applause didn't shake the house by a long shot. Through the random rather desultory clapping, and the craning of necks, rose a couple of catcalls and not a few sounds which were even more derogatory. C. D. Taylor, one of the Goldfield's tallest men in natural talent if not experience and a gent who'd forgotten more about mining than most of those present could ever hope to pick up, peered at Scoop in disgust. "You taken leave of your senses?"

"I don't think so," Featherstone smiled. "That's a man your grandkids — and maybe theirs, too — will probably read about in —"

"That," Taylor said, "is Henry Clay Jenkens, the dadburndest deadbeat and blowhard —"

"Now, jest a dang minute!" Slim cried, looking ugly. "I don't have to take that! Not from you nor nobody! You denyin', by godfreys, I discovered the Mammoth?"

"I ain't denying you sold Carltenmore a 'claim' for three hundred dollars — only piece of ground you ever had title to. But that don't make it the Mammoth. Nor a lot of hot air from an out-of-work newshound don't make you no kind of mogul in *my* book!" Taylor owned the faulted Jumbo, from which he'd already taken about a million and a quarter. As a long-time member of the steering committee he considered the threatened inclusion of a pipsqueak like Jenkens little short of downright blasphemy. "Why," he said, affronted and outraged, "that walloper . . ."

Taylor hadn't run out of either breath or scorn. But Scoop, just the same, had grabbed the play away from him — by the simple expedient of dropping a chunk of gold ore on the bar. Grinning smugly he said, "Have a look at that, boys."

Every man there was already looking, including C. D. Taylor, whose jaw must have dropped a foot and forty inches. "Where'd that come from?" he said suspiciously.

"Just a sample," Scoop grinned, "of what's still underground if a man's got the fortitude to get out and hunt for it. Slim fetched it in from his new claim this evening. Brought a whole sack —"

"More likely stole, if you want my opinion!" Taylor irascibly said.

"Harsh words, C.D. But I *would* like to have your opinion," Scoop declared. "As a man who knows mining inside and out, how much would you say this will run to the ton?"

"He won't get no ton!"

"But say he should?" Scoop persisted, and the Jumbo's owner took a long look around.

"Such a fuss over nothing. This whole thing's ridiculous! Don't you know picked rock when you look at it? That's the same kind of thing he palmed off on Ezra —"

A commotion at the back of the room fell apart to the sudden forward thrust of bull moose shoulders; and a gleaming hippo-shaped head appeared above the ruck of startled, turning faces. This huge leviathan rolled through the crowd with the force of a tidal wave, coming to rest at the bar alongside the reporter where the shrewd, piggish eyes briefly inspected Scoop's exhibit then plowed straight to Jenkens' face. In that crammed-still quiet you could have heard a mouse blink.

Carltenmore showed his expensive dentures in what was intended to be an affable smile. "Congratulations, Slim," he said like Moses handing down the Twelve Commandments. "I rejoice in your luck and applaud the fruits of your conniving zeal. But then I knew you could do it," and he looked at Slim fondly. "Of all my boys I had the most faith in you. I was telling Mrs. C. just the other —"

Jenkens, glowering, said, "You can tie that bull outside. I ain't one of your 'boys' an' I don't owe you a cent — not a golrammed penny!"

Carltenmore quizzically rubbed a raised brow. "In all the excitement of striking it rich perhaps you've forgotten we have a grubstake agreement —"

"The word's 'had'," Slim growled, "an' you dang well know it! That arrangement run out a year ago last week." He dug a grimy paper from a pocket of his vest, pulled the creases apart and triumphantly slapped it down on the bar. "Take a squint at that date!"

Scoop picked it up, took a look and passed it on. "He's right."

But Ezra P. didn't seem much perturbed. More in sorrow than in anger he took up the chunk of ore, hefted it in his hand a couple times and tossed it back on the bar. "At least you'll admit —"

"Ain't admittin' a thing!"

Carltenmore grinned. "Your privilege. But that doesn't change the facts, my boy. I know you fetched this ore into town. I have the whole lot, every chunk you brought, including that piece you traded the Mohawk for the grub you put into you. I've had it analyzed and, while it's obviously picked rock, it is equally plain it came out of a mine. So in front of these witnesses I'll ask you to make good on the IOU's you plastered this town with. I've got them right here," he said, tapping a bulging pocket. "They tote up to twenty-three hundred, forty-seven dollars and fifty-eight cents." He said, soft as spider steps, "You going to redeem them?"

Slim's face was a study in frustrated anger. Scoop Featherstone's pencil was racing over the lined pad on his knee; nobody else moved so much as a muscle. "Hell's fire!" Slim yelled, so mad he was shaking. "You think I carry around that kinda cash!"

"The point is not what I think but what you, Mr. Jenkens, are prepared to do about it." He brought the notes from his pocket. "These call for payment on demand." He stacked them on the bar and set Scoop's rock on top of them. "I've been to a lot of trouble —"

"Yeah," said Slim bitterly. "Keeps me up nights feelin' sorry about you! That how-come you shut up your mine? So's you'd have more time t' go snoopin' around, threatenin' people, buyin' up bills —"

"I took up these notes because it seemed pretty certain I was dealing with a man who couldn't be trusted. A cheapjack crook who never intended to meet his obli—"

Slim yelled, "Why, dang your eyes, I —"

"What do you call that eight hundred dollars you said you had to have to open up the vein?" Carltenmore shifted his mountain of flesh. "I'm a business man, Slim, but I try to be fair. Now, isn't it true that when you took my money you promised solemnly to share with me half of anything you found? Yes or no?"

"No!" shouted Jenkens, looking about to jump plumb out of his clothes. "You never *give* me any money! Never *was* no vein! What the hell are you —"

Carltenmore threw up his hands.

You probably couldn't have found three persons in the place who did not believe he was a hoodwinked man. He seemed about to reach for Scoop's sample again but,

74

wryly shrugging, turned back, sadly shaking his head. Anyone could see it was a piece of mined ore.

He said with admirable patience, "It isn't just the money, it's the principle of the thing. A man's got a right to protect his investment. Still, I'll give you a choice. Pay back what you owe me or fight it out in the courts."

"I'll —"

"Wait!" Peremptorily Carltenmore held up a hand. "Your indebtedness now is a matter of public record. Before you go off half-cocked and start shouting, I think you should know that if we go into court it might tie the mine up for as much as twenty years. Is that what you want? Can you afford such an action?"

He stood back, blandly smiling; and Slim came out of his trance with a hoot. "*What* mine!" he jeered.

Ezra P. showed his teeth. "You'll have to do better than that. My reports — Don't be ridiculous! That ore speaks for itself. It came out of a *mine*."

"All right," Slim said, grinning. "Go ahead and find it."

And he laughed all the way back to the hotel.

VII

The recurrent vision of Carltenmore's face was balm to Jenkens' revenge-hungry soul. The danged old rip had been so sure, so patronizingly confident he had his victim where the hair was short and would skin him again out of what stacked up to be a fabulous fortune, Slim sat enthroned in tears of joy just remembering the hate of those shaved hog features. What a gut-buster! Golly Moses!

But in the midst of this six-beer celebration a corrosive thought creeping through his skull slanched a thickening disquiet across Slim's triumph. The head of Mammoth Mines, Inc. was not one to relish the short end of a deal. Most distinctly he wasn't the kind to yell *Boo* at.

Ezra P. was a power in the land, and one who could shake a mighty big stick. No one had got the best of him yet and all the weight of his displeasure would be marshaled to blast a man brash enough to try.

In this sobering reflection Slim quickened with alarm.

Scowling, he got up and began to tramp

the rooms. The suite seemed suddenly, oppressively close — a whole heap too close to Ezra P. for comfort. Slim had no more hankering to get roughed up than any other feller if the thing could be avoided; and the more he considered it the more convinced he became that the hereafter of this might get very rough indeed. Carltenmore's rep as a winner was at stake, not to mention the bait Slim had been at such pains to dangle under his nose.

The danged old hypothecator was likely closeted right now with Hell Creek Charlie, honing up their axes and polishing final details aimed at putting H. C. Jenkens so deep under ground not even the goddamn worms would find him!

He sleeved the sweat off paling cheeks and tried to scoff the thought away. But the truth was that while Ezra, maybe, wouldn't stick his neck out quite so far, all bets was off when it came to Charlie. He was a murderin' son of a bitch for sure! Without Carltenmore's pull he'd have been strung up long ago.

Jenkens eased open the hall door for a look, then caught up his hat and set out for the stairs. If this was the day for cashing in chips he meant to take his where they couldn't be got hold of.

Which was considerable easier said than done.

He got the mule all right, slapped on the gear and stepped into the saddle. Then a vision of the Carltenmore hardcase, Hell Creek, settled between the crotch of his ears and set him to thinking about the long miles ahead which a man would have to cover if he hoped to feel safe. Regrets wouldn't butter any great amount of parsnips, but he couldn't help wishing he'd played the hand a little different. Sort of strung it out and not tamped so much blue lightning into the hole of Carltenmore's pride.

By now the story would be all over town how that crazy dang desert rat Death Valley Slim, had tapped the mother lode, bearded his patron in the Goldfield Club Bar and tied the big man's tail in a knot. And about this time tomorrow, or the next day, if H. C. Jenkens wasn't almighty careful, they were like to be reading how that dadburned fool had got overtook by a horrible tragedy some place out in the sage and sand.

He dared not stay and he was scared to go.

If he could just reach Stovepipe Wells or Furnace Creek, or pretty near any other part of Death Valley, he could thumb his nose at the whole durn pack. He was ready for 'em there! But the problem right now was getting over the line, getting to where he had defenses set up.

Back at his ranch over in Bearclaw Canyon it had seemed like he'd thought of just about everything but he sure hadn't thought to be on the run *this* quick. There was three or four other things had slipped his mind, but the big thing was Charlie, the Carltenmore hardcase, who wouldn't no more mind bustin' a hole through a feller than he would about swattin' a gol-rammed fly!

The corpsemaker. The Roy Horn of Nevader. That was what they called him out among the rimrocks when they wanted to be extry polite. Like if there was some woman around.

Till they found where the gold was they probably wouldn't go so far as to outright kill him, but there was things in this world could make a death a real blessin'. And one of them was Charlie. If he was in town, or any place word from Ezra could reach him, the trails was probably watched right now!

There was several ways into the valley from Nevada. You could get in around

Quartzite over Deadman's Pass, but that was too far south — and the same went for Kelley's Well. You could drop down from Rhyolite by way of Chloride City or Daylight Pass, but Jenkens just now was a long piece from that place and Gretchen, his mule, had ought to be reshod. And she had better be rested up some if they were going to make time and stay clear of Carltenmore's scouts.

You could slip in from Leadville via Titus Canyon, but unless a man came onto it through Rhyolite from Beatty he'd need a cast-iron hide and a heap more luck than Slim had even the faintest right to look for. Which left only Lida and the Grapevine Canyon road direct from Goldfield, and they'd be camped on these if they wasn't no place else.

A worm could have made better time than he was making now. All the weight of the world seemed hung round his shoulders and the mule, too, looked to have got a bellyful of travel. When it finally got through to him Gretchen had quit and was standing there half asleep on her feet, Slim really got the wind up. No one but a nump would dream of tackling that desert in no better shape than this — but he hadn't no other choice. If they picked him up, if he fell into Charlie's hands . . .

Slim looked around wildly, unable for a moment to orient himself in this maze of back alleys, so engrossed had he become trying to think his way past a situation that should have been foreseen before he started. Then, sharp against the town's illumination, he spied the dark top of a distant schoolhouse and realized he had wandered into one of the most disreputable parts of town — not the crib district, actually, but an area given over to the lowest paid help of the mining hierarchy. Shantytown. A patchwork of tents and packing crates, flapping tin and naked brats, a warren where a throat could be cut for two bits — and, just as this fact settled into his consciousness, somewhere in the dark a woman screamed.

Between his knees the mule stiffened into an ears-back squat. She was snuffling the wind, plumb ready to go, when Jenkens' own stabbing eyes, fiercely raking the gloom, took hold of a moving deeper clot in the piled-up shadows between the two nearest shacks.

"You there!" he yelled, ripping the pistol out of his shirt. And without more ado, he leapt from his saddle and went plunging headlong into the murk. The woman cried out again. Muzzle flame tore from a reared-up shape. Slim's legs went flying out from under him, and the next thing he had any real assurance of he was plowing up dirt with the scoop of his chin, while off through the night thumped a garble of fading boot sound.

The villain was gone, fled away in the dark. Coming onto all fours, Slim half believed his jaw was gone too, scrubbed away on the rasp of the gravelly soil. The girl helped him up. She was too slight, he thought, to be a full-bodied woman — not that it made any difference to Slim! All females, to his mind, spelled nothing but trouble. It was her he'd fell over and he could, just as well, have broken his gol-rammed neck.

"What the hell was you doin' down there!" he spluttered, gingerly fingering the ache in his throat. "Who was that guy, anyhow? Was he botherin' you?"

"*No le hace*. I am safe," she said through her panting. "God will repay him." She tugged at her blouse, tried to shake some of the dust out of her ankle-length skirt. He caught himself staring. It was too dark where they stood for Slim to make out more than the blob of her face, but, as she shyly attempted to express appreciation for his timely intervention, there was something about her that seemed vaguely familiar. Almost as though he'd been through this before. . . .

Then he knew.

He sure had! It was that Mexican witch Dolores Ramirez, the gambusino's daughter, that he had yesterday saved from Ezra's lecherous super and that knife cuddling stope boss!

And Slim shook off her hand and jumped back with a curse.

VIII

It was hard — powerful hard — not to fling himself onto his mule and take straightaway out for the hills like a twister. Each remembered experience warned him fiercely against her, not to mention the loco things she'd said yesterday or the goosing look of that flat-faced Tomas, whipping out a pig-sticker just because Slim wasn't about to climb into double harness with nobody!

Drawn back, coldly sweating, Jenkens peered at her again. He didn't need to see much; he remembered she was young, but baby rattlers was, too, and purely as poisonous mean as the rest of them! She was practically an Injun — half Injun, anyhow. He got the shakes in his knees just thinking about it.

But there was worse things than Injuns. Alongside Charlie even a hydrophoby skunk could look good. He rubbed his hands on his pant's legs. Breaking into her talk he said, tense and gruff, "Can you hide me?"

She turned. He could feel the dig of her probing stare. "*¿Qué?* What did you say?"

84

Jenkens shifted uneasily, remembering now that they were after her, too — same tribe anyway. But it was the best chance he had; they'd have every hole in the border stuffed by this time. They was bound to have discovered he had quit the Esmeralda.

He said, clearing his throat, "I've got to hide out a spell."

She stared some more, bent and picked something up. Standing there, fingering it, he could feel her eyes searching him. Something else caught his attention. "That my gun?"

She shook her head. "It is the *medicamento* — the medicine. For my father. From the mines he has the cough. All the time he has it. Come!"

Slim found his gun, thrust it inside his shirt and, catching up Gretchen's reins, trailed her off through the night rather bitterly wondering if he might, after all, better have taken his chances with Ezra's scouts.

She must have been nearly home because, in less than five minutes they slipped out of the last of several dark alleys and came up to a shed drunkenly leaning against a solid wall of adobes ten feet high. To Slim it looked like the end of the line.

The girl, stepping into this ramshackle structure, motioned him after her. "Fetch the mule," she whispered, and abruptly disappeared.

Gretchen, laying back her ears, made ready to take root, only Slim was too quick for her. He didn't much like the looks of this himself, but wasn't about to let a mule get the best of him — not, by godfreys, Henry Clay Jenkens!

He had the surprised Gretchen half into the rickety leanto before, with frightened indignation, she braced and balked. Jenkens managed to shove the rest of her in. By throwing her off-balance he was able eventually to shut and fasten the whoppy-jawed door.

"Over here," the girl called through the dust and confusion and, feeling his stumbling way toward her voice Slim found the laid-up wall was not the blind passage he'd imagined. A heavy oak door, concealed within the shed and which Dolores fastened after them, let into a kind of patio where a fountain gurgled beneath a pair of scraggly peppers that looked old enough to have been put out by Noah. In the heavy gloom, whose only illumination lemonly seeped from the twinkling blanket of overhead stars, he was vaguely aware of several recumbent shapes deployed on pallets against a far wall.

The girl said softly, "Don't wake the little ones," and, taking his hand, towed him past the sleepers to a second door which disclosed, when opened, the feeble glow of a low-turned lamp. In the fringe of this radiance a man lay, propped with lumpy pillows, in a tilt-backed chair. His sunken cheeks seemed flushed, his eyes fever bright. There was a wasted look about his loose frame which spoke of lost flesh, and his big-knuckled hands clenched the chair arms like talons. Looking into those eyes Jenkens had the notion his most secret thoughts were undergoing scrutiny.

The girl said, "*Papá,* this is Don Enriqué," and went off into a clatter of excitable Spanish spoken too fast for Slim to keep up with, though he did latch onto enough to get the drift. She was bragging him up for the courage and promptness with which, not only yesterday but again this very night, he had saved her from *los molestars.* It was while the old man was adding his felicitations and thanks to the uproar that Slim, somewhat flustered, discovered Tomas with his lip curled sitting back in the room-corner shadows.

"My poor house is yours," the father, Elfego, said courteously in Spanish. "Please excuse me for not rising to greet you properly, *señor,* but I have not been myself of late. I have a sickness here," he said, touching his chest, "but you will be welcome under this roof for as long as it pleases you to stay."

Jenkens, grunting, could see this did not sit well with the girl's oldest brother. The boy's look was sullen and his handsome face held the fixedness of hate.

The father said, "Dolores, bring some of the little cakes for our friend, and a bottle of the red Hermosillo." Slim would have passed this, for the hour was late, but Elfego would not hear of it. He had his pride and Dolores, it seemed, was the apple of his eye. Nothing was too much trouble which might show their appreciation to the preserver of her virtue.

So the lamp was turned up and they wined and dined on the sweets she had made and the fruit of the grape, with much Spanish rhetoric thrown in for good measure. It was pretty near daylight when the girl showed Slim a place to bed down. Like enough it was the only true bed in the house, a hugely massive four-poster. It looked old enough — all them billows and flounces, to have sailed with H. Cortez, Menendez, or some other long-whiskered freebooter, its queer-looking wood elaborately encrusted with cherubs and a miscellany of double-breasted females as plumb bare naked as Beelzebub's harem!

Kind of made Slim blush just to look at the thing; and, quick as she left, he blew out the candle and hauled off his boots. Reluctantly, as a further concession to what might be expected of a gent in a Christian home like this, he got out of his vest — even took off his shirt, but the pistol went snugly under his pillow.

He had the dangdest dreams. The worst and most vivid was someway tangled and tied to Dolores. Seemed like him and her had took off some place on some crazy damn trip he never did get the straight of. Every time they got to where it looked like he might be able to draw a full breath, up bobbed Tomas coming hell-bent for Slim with that goddamn knife slashing hell west and crooked! It didn't make no difference what Slim said — nor all Dolores' piety nor tears; Tomas wasn't settling for anything short of Slim's sweat-soaked scalp. Only chance Slim had was to get clean out of Nevada, but Tomas had lined up all Slim's enemies and there were bushwhackers camped on every trail. Once they pretty near nailed him for sure; only the mule's startled snort had got him clear.

And then she was down with Slim plowing chin-first through the clutch of catclaw, and Tomas with his knife scarce a hand's length behind.

Slim woke, snarling, wet as though he'd been in a river, with the bedclothes all twisted round his neck. He squirmed loose of the grip someone had on his shoulder and, looking wild-eyed up, found Tomas' face rather nastily regarding him.

Slim guessed he must be still in the dream; then decided he wasn't as the boy — he could hardly be more than scarcely into his teens — bent nearer to say in irascible Spanish, "Speak, Red Rat, and talk once from the heart. Is it not God's truth you came here but to hide?"

Jenkens threw off the covers and, grunting, reached for a boot. He stood up, stamping into it, ignoring the lad. He stomped into the other and looked for his shirt.

Tomas cried angrily, "We are not peons! She would not come empty handed — Look at me, gringo!"

The boy in a dream was one thing. In the flesh he was nothing but a golrammed nuisance and Jenkens, eying him, snorted with contempt.

"I think," Tomas shouted, "you have

never thought to marry our sister!"

"Outa the mouths of babes," Slim said with a laugh, and caught up his chin-strapped straw and sloshed it on. He got into his shirt, tucked in the tails and, oddly enough, discovered Tomas smiling, too, *mui mucho malévolo*. Like the cat grinning round the tail of the goldfinch.

With an unpleasant laugh the boy strode to the window, peering into the street. Then he threw up the sash. "In here, *hombres!*"

Jenkens took one look and ran from the room.

IX

Without the girl's help he'd have been trapped for sure, but love — the real kind — is never asleep. It is not resentful, self-seeking or mean. It asks only to serve and, hearing the shouts and clamor from the street, Elfego's willow-slim daughter, putting all else aside, came on wings of the wind to whisk him away while the Grubstake King's henchmen were scrambling in through the window.

By empty rooms and weed-grown lots, through walls of stone, barred gates and goat runs, they fled in the evening's deepening gloom to where she had tethered his trusty mule.

Slim leaped to the saddle and would have gone straightaway without so much as a parting glance, but the girl grabbed the cheek strap and fetched him up short. "Turn loose!" he yelled in a lather of impatience. "What you tryin' t' do — git me kilt?"

Dolores, coloring a little, let go of the bridle. "It's only — well, here!" she said, reaching out and up.

Jenkens stared. You'd have thought by his look, she was trying to hand him a squirming varmint instead of the gun he'd left under his pillow. You would have reckoned a girl as pretty as her might get a word of grudging thanks.

But not from him!

Too well he knew that moon-struck glance, those parted lips, the awful curse of his fatal charm. He snatched the six-shooter, flapped spurred heels, and took off south in a cloud of dust.

He never looked back. He had long since learned even a semblance of decency, the barest bones of appreciation, could be swallowed whole for plighted troth and haul a man straight up to the altar. The mule's namesake had taught him that. Big-nosed Gretchen of the whiskered lip whose bearhug holds had mighty near taken him down for the count!

But it *was* dang queer, her having that gun. He dug it out of his shirt and scowled at it, baffled. There had hardly been time for her to get near the bed and he distinctly remembered shoving it under the pillow before he'd pulled up the covers. To be sure, while he'd slept, that scrinch-eyed brother might of made off with it to be on the safe side in what he'd tried later.

Slim shook his head, still fighting his hat. He changed the loads and, still scowling, put the pistol away. There was things more urgent to be wrassled with now, like how to break clear of Charlie's scouts at the border. Nobody had to look into his palm for Slim to know that would take considerable doing. It wasn't much likely they'd been called off yet.

It occurred to him he might have took off too quick, that he'd probably been smarter to have dug in at the hotel. Ezra P., as head of Mammoth Mines, had face to watch out for; he couldn't afford to have the word get around that folks who crossed him might turn up full of bullets.

Slim guessed he'd done right. Accidents could happen and, when a guy tangled with Charlie, they generally did. There was that feller Haines who'd fell under a wagon. And Cully Stokes who'd got kicked by a horse. Old Man Fletcherson that they claimed had stumbled into a open shaft. Most vivid of all though, in Slim's remembrance, was crusty Mac Jones — a plain case of lead poisonin', the coroner said.

It was full dark again. Blacker, by grab, than a stack of shined stove lids. The wind crying round him felt downright chilly

Slim noticed, peering about, and reached again to make sure he still had the pistol.

They would sure as hell be watching the trail through Lida. The obvious route, because it was nearest, would be Grapevine Canyon that forked and went on southeast to the Wells or, via Grapevine Springs to Hidden Valley. Once he passed Tin Mountain there wasn't a Injun on Carltenmore's payroll that couldn't be made a fool of; and Charlie's scouts would reason if he'd been going that way he would have showed last night.

That made it look pretty good. Like dollars to doughnuts if there was watchers still there they'd probably already have quit straining their eyes. Jenkens stopped to call heads and flipped one of his gold pieces, then couldn't read the dang thing when he grabbed it. He turned Gretchen anyway, and cut for the canyon.

They could see well enough once the sky filled with stars. Wasn't nothing to look at but sagebrush anyhow. Sage and sand. A few odds and ends of cactus that who the hell wanted to look at anyway? Nothing so big as a house or a tree. Hard to see what the Injuns had made such a row about.

He was thankful the moon was in its last quarter. It would be late getting up and, by pushing the mule, there was just a bare chance he might get by the watch point before those on guard knew the quarry was onto them. A lot depended, of course, on where the thing was set up. In the Nevada end of the canyon probably, Jenkens thought, squinting again at the stars. The next hour or so would likely tell the tale.

His gut was beginning to gnaw at him again, adding its ache to his other harassments. He could see the deeper dark of the Last Chance Range off there to the right, and dead south a spell where them stars was wiped out would be the spread-out bulk of the Cottonwood Mountains and beyond, the Panamints, that some places went straight up through the clouds.

With the country turning rapidly rougher and Gretchen grunting from the twist of the grades Slim slid off to follow her tail, feeling the wind hard against his face. The sage was gone, left behind on the flats; the air he got now, stinking hard of fried rocks, was being channeled up out of Death Valley. And now the burnt smell was stronger, pretty near overpowering. Mighty soon, watching Gretchen's ears, Jenkens stopped, filled with disquiet, to listen and stare at the blue-gray shadows while his heart thumped loudly under its burden of suspicion.

Moving once more, he pushed the mule on ahead of him, watching her carefully, pausing when she paused, probing the dark with the stab of bleak glance. It damned well smelled like brush fires to him; and where the walls of the canyon reached their narrowest point the smell was so rank he got down on all fours and started feeling around, sniffing and snuffling with muttered obscenities. At last he stood up, not satisfied really but at any rate convinced.

Charlie's Injuns were gone — but not too long ago, either. This was the place they had figured to stop him. Stretched clean across both flanks of the road was the ashes of their fires, some of them still warm. Two nights they'd been camped here, crouched over their rifles, waiting for him to walk into their sights. If he hadn't laid over with Elfego Ramirez —

Jenkens pushed that thought away from him, sleeving the cold damp off his cheeks. He put his pistol away and got back on the mule.

By the time first light began to thin out the shadows he had Tin Mountain off to the left and was walking again to keep up Gretchen's strength. There was a spring off the trail a piece about an hour farther south, and if he could make it that far before his backbone rubbed clean through to his navel he reckoned he'd survive.

He didn't make as good time as he'd thought he would. It was shank deep on ten when he quit the road and struck off across some pretty rough country that, if he hadn't completely missed his bearings, had ought to connect with Hidden Valley, which was where he was making out to ranch these days.

Gretchen was some gaunted when they finally hove in sight of the spring, and the first thing she did when Slim got the saddle off was put down her nose and start lipping the water. The pool was lower than Slim remembered it, but with the drought still on he wasn't much surprised. He looked around for tracks and, not finding any, dug grub and grain from the cache he'd hidden back in the rocks. Pretty soon they were both busy stuffing their guts, the mule with cracked oats, Slim with black jerky washed down with tomatoes.

It was while he was searching his pockets afterwards to see how many double eagles he had left that Jenkens came across the rubberbanded colored papers. He'd no recollection of having seen them before, but he got the message quick enough once he'd opened and spread out a couple. They were stock certificates, mostly Sandstorm — the mine that had been dumping that queer looking ore. Three hundred, five hundred . . . Time he thumbed through them he found himself holding twenty-four hundred and eighty-seven shares of a hole in the ground that not even its leasers had any more faith in.

He reckoned that feller Reilly had really latched onto him.

Standing there with the proof of it Slim didn't have to wonder what had happened to the sack of samples he'd fetched in or how they had got into Carltenmore's hands. Yet he didn't lift half the hell you'd have looked for in a man so bad taken.

Oh, he cussed some and slammed around a few things and pretty near at one point fed the whole batch to that earwaggling mule. But in the end he stuffed them all back in his pockets and even, in a kind of wry way, laughed a little. His gorgeous specimens were gone, but they were not forgotten; and just to make sure doubly certain he reckoned pretty soon he'd better sack up some more.

Where a little was good, more was bound to be better, and Ezra wasn't half worked up enough yet.

X

When he got back to the boar's nest — Slim's own term for the homestead he occasionally put in some time at — there was chores piled up enough to take him a week if a man had a mind to get down and grapple with them.

What he needed was a helper. His thoughts jumped straight to the Ramirez girl and, just as quick, got themselves cuffed hell west and crooked. Maybe she wasn't no big-beak Gretchen but she was dang sure female, and that was enough for Slim. Why, he'd sooner keep a live lion round the place as to get himself saddled with any female woman! Even the bare notion proved too much to put up with, and he went out and caught up his second-string mule and set off straightaway to find him a Injun.

Best place for that — nearest, anyhow — was Stovepipe Wells which if a man didn't mind clamberin' over the Panamints, he could get to by a hit-or-miss trail that straddled the length of Cottonwood Canyon and crawled out through the dunes about ten miles from the place.

Jenkens didn't wait even to stop for a breather. While he wasn't about to admit it, what he really was trying to get caught up with was some nerve-wrenching distraction fierce and shattering enough to drive every memory of her out of his head.

Which was easier looked for than found, he discovered. Getting onto that trail from where he was at could be guaranteed to make a heap of folks yell for a calf rope. Though Slim was copiously sweating time he got to the springs that marked the start of the trail, the scary cliffs and drops he'd been forced to negotiate hadn't even put a curl in his hair. It was them goddamn visions he kept having of Dolores.

Never was a man more bedeviled by re-membrances, and gnashing his teeth didn't help him none, neither. After all the com-motions he'd had account of women, you would think, by grab, a feller'd have more control. Or at least pick someone big enough to catch a hold on!

He stood himself to a splashing bath while the mule stared like he had gone off his rocker. When Jenkens fisted a stone the critter backed off some, but the things in Slim's head wasn't amenable to threats and he threw on his clothes in a frustration of cursing.

He got over the Panamints before dark caught him, but there was still better than fifteen miles of canyon travel before he could expect to get into the sandhills, and he'd come away again without either grub or rifle. He cussed some more while he let the mule blow, and then he hiked a few miles but that didn't help noticeably. He got back in the saddle and put some more miles behind him.

It was plain enough now he wasn't going to make that sand before daybreak and, even crowding the mule, maybe not short of noon. Seemed like he might just as well try to get in a little shut-eye. So at the first decent campsite he got down, pulled his rig and, with the mule's sweaty blanket to ward off a chill, curled himself up — after stompin' around some to scare off the snakes — in the lee of a boulder.

The sun was an hour past noon when he woke, and it could have been later if the mule hadn't roused him trying to get at some branches. Zachary Taylor was the handle Slim had given him, and there was some resemblance, he being the kind of critter that despised fuss and feathers; he was fearless, too, and ignorant and good-natured. He could fend for himself, having never been pampered, and was sufficiently independent, had the notion struck him, he could just as well have ambled off and left Slim afoot. So the first thing Slim did, once he grasped the situation, was to clap the hackamore on him and tether him with its cotton rope, after which he stood a while sorting his problems.

At least he didn't have to worry, for a spell anyway, about Hell Creek Charlie and his Shoshoni scouts. If they hadn't given up they were probably still hunkered around Sand Spring off west of Gold Mountain waiting for Slim to walk into their trap.

The sun was far over the Harrisburg Flats and canting to drop back of Telescope Peak when he rode into the Wells. The Panamints, shifted around to the right of him, were tan and dun and rose with lavender overtones and in all that wild expanse of country the only sign of motion came from a dust devil careening through the white glare of windwhipped sand.

In front of the bottle house, across from the pump, Jenkens stepped from the mule and, ducking his head, moved into the dugout some enterprising outlander a couple or three years ago had set up here alongside the freight road between Skidoo and Rhyolite with the Yankee notion of dispensing drinks and trinkets. He appeared well-fed standing back of his counter looking Jenkens over in the symphony of colors sun-shoved through the bottle walls. "How!" he said, bringing up a paw in the Injun peace sign.

There was a kind of queer look about the corners of his mouth and he was sure powerful long on stare but Slim, who figured all foreigners to be a little tetched anyhow, said, like he was still outdoors trying to shout down the wind, "I'll take a beer."

His words slammed against the glass walls like ricocheting blue whistlers while the factotum of this establishment, a good twenty years ahead of his tourist-trap colleagues, stepped out back to dig up a bottle. Returning, wiping off the sand against a red-gartered shirtsleeve, the proprietor inquired, "Taking it with you or drinking it here?"

"Here," Slim said, "if you don't mind knockin' the neck off."

"That'll be a dollar," the man grumbled, prizing off the cap.

His continued inspection was getting under Slim's skin, but the beer was cool and Jenkens smacked his lips. With his glance skipping over the miscellany of Injun gewgaws taking up a generous seven-eighths of the space, he said, "This stuff for sale?"

"That's right, friend. Anything you see. If you don't see it, name it. We can probably get it. What did you have in mind?"

"An Injun," Slim grinned, and the fat man looked at him harder than ever. Rubbing his jowls, still staring, he said in a voice barely robust enough to make the trek, "Gov'ment's taking a dim view of that lately. Claim it stirs up trouble, so much used goods going back on the tribes. Nothing personal, of course, but —"

Red-necked, Jenkens explained he wasn't talking about females.

"Oh, then you're in luck," the fat man beamed. "Bunch of bucks due in here just about dusk. Say! Your name ain't Jenkens, is it?"

"An' if it is?" Slim said, dropping into a crouch.

The businessman blinked, hesitantly clearing his throat. "Some fellers here asking for you a while back —"

"How far back, an' what fellers?"

The fat proprietor looked as though he regretted having mentioned it. He wasn't too foreign to miss the menace in Slim's stance. He said, reluctantly, "Albino. Scoop-jawed, sort of gangling. Eye like a gimlet."

There wasn't no red in Jenkens' neck now. "Scowls like a bloodhound? Bullhide chaps?"

"That's him," the man nodded.

Slim put down the beer. "He have some Shoshonies with him?"

"Four fellers. Indians — can't say what kind. To me all redskins look alike."

"I expect," Slim said, "he wanted to know where I live. What'd you tell him?"

"Told him far as I knew I'd never met up with you."

"If he comes back," Slim said, "you tell him I moved. You ain't sure where but you heard it was some place south of Furnace Creek, which is where I'll be goin' when I pull outa here." He eyed the guy, scowling. "When you reckon them Injuns'll pop up?"

The fat man stepped over to the door and peered out. "Hadn't ought to be long. They show up, generally, while I'm fryin' my supper."

Jenkens wooled that around, debating the wisdom of waiting at all with Hell Creek casting so close for sign. Then the cheek of the bugger coming clean over here got to riding Slim's sense of the fitness of things. His brows pulled down and he hunched up his shoulders like a mule in a hailstorm.

He became so indignant he forgot his fright. All he could think of was the arrogant insolence of Carltenmore's hatchetman invading what in all conscience were Jenkens' own stomping grounds. High time, Slim thought, someone laid off to learn that flame-spewin' son a few of the hornier facts of life!

And who was better able than Henry Clay Jenkens? Nobody knew this country like he did. Why, for two cents, by grab, he would toll that pinto-vested whippoorwill so deep into its wastes not even the U.S. Army could find him!

But right in the midst of this fussing and fuming the boil of Slim's bile began to cool off a little. He wasn't quite fixed yet to tangle with Charlie. He still had a lot more cans to get planted before he could afford to stick his neck out that far. Whatever else you might say about him Hell Creek *was* rough. Corpses strewn all over his backtrail, excused or forgotten by grace of King Ezra's wealth and influence.

But the combination wasn't unbeatable. No cover was so good you couldn't find a chink in it. There was a blazing hereafter for them and their kind; but it was hard, bitter hard, to have to wait for the day.

Boldness was needed but the risks must be counted.

XI

For the next pair of weeks H. C. Jenkens spent so much of his time on muleback his work-grimed Levi's — the two times he got out of them — crouched stiff in their tracks as the bowlegged pants to a conquistador's suit.

It was a shocking sight to see those once-blue jeans acting like they still had somebody in them. Rigid as boards, without boots or belly, they hung poised on their cuffs with the cant of a cutting horse keyed-up for action. The squat Paiute fetched by Slim from the Wells appeared considerably impressed — even nervously so if one could judge by the beads of sweat they broke out of him. Slim pretty near worked himself into a stupor but at the end of the fortnight he had everything ready.

"Flinch Eye," he said, as they rode back to the ranch, "this is a miserable world an' you better believe it. Tomorrow I'm takin' a *pasear* over to Goldfield, an' while I'm gone you're boss of the outfit. You with me this far?"

The Indian grunted.

"All right." Slim lifted the rifle — a .45-90 — out of the sling where it hung from his saddle. "You savvy 'present'? Good enough. You keep — all time yours, from now till stars never shine no more — your gun," and he put the heavy rifle into the hungry copper hands. "Never mind what color, I don't want nobody prowlin' this place while I'm away. *Nobody*. You got that?"

The Paiute's eyes glittered. "Sure. Me killum."

Slim considered him, hesitant, then jerked a nod. "That's it. You see anything, you shoot. *Andale — pronto!*"

Meantime, back in Goldfield business had recovered from its threatened lapse and the boom was expanding in every direction. The railroad had been extended, and the arrival of the line's first train in town, with no less a personage than Governor Sparks aboard, had set off a celebration from which a number of nabobs were still hung over. The price of lots soared. Stone and brick buildings were springing up all over. It sure enough looked to be a genuine metropolis, its residences spreading far out across the desert. The market had jumped to an all-time high, the tickers were unraveling reams of tape and all wires to the Exchange were jammed with a spate of orders to buy. Harried brokers were yanking their hair out by handfuls; they couldn't secure enough shares to half fill the demand. Even the phonies being launched by the crooks were snatched up as fast as certificates could be fetched from the printers. And this wasn't just local. The widows and bank clerks had gone screaming crazy; any fool name you might slap on a paper would sell if seen over a bright Goldfield dateline.

The newshounds were back in full force. Featherstone's scoop on Death Valley Slim had returned him to favor with his East Coast employers. His wages were tripled, his stuff syndicated to less fortunate dailies. He was filing copy every night, covering the latest Goldfield developments, liberally seasoned with tongue-in-cheek allusions to that Midas of Death Valley Henry Clay Jenkens, most of which came straight out of his head.

Much of this was picked up and re-hashed in other rags. Some of the wilder stories dribbled back to be refurbished with fanfare by Jimmy O'Brien in the Goldfield *News*. Carltenmore, furious, was more than half minded to call in Charlie to straighten him out, might even have done it had he known where to reach him. But the desert had swallowed his pet leather slapper; there had been no reports in the past seven days.

Nor was this all that appeared out of joint to King Ezra. The reports from his assayer had thrown him badly off his feed. Jenkens' samples — the sack of them Carltenmore had purchased from Reilly — looked suspiciously like his own ore from the Mammoth. It had every characteristic — only more so, assaying at least twice as much to the ton. His man declared vehemently it *was* Mammoth ore, but Ezra, sweating with greed and these intolerable suspicions, still refused to believe. "That don't make sense. It's preposterous, damn it! How could he get it? Not an ounce has gone out since the Jumbo faulted. I've got enough guards —"

"You asked for my opinion."

"But a mouse couldn't get past that cordon of guns!"

"Maybe he grabbed it before —"

"Poppycock!" Ezra snorted. "If that was the case why hold off till now? The man hasn't had any cash in three years! My spies have assured me —"

"I'm not talking about spies. Metals are

my business, and I tell you this stuff," he said, slapping the sack, "gives every indication of coming off the same vein. In fact," he growled, adamant, "it came out of your mine. I'll testify to that in any court in the land!"

Carltenmore glared. The assayer glared back. "At least," Ezra wheedled, "you won't deny it *could* have come from some other vein?"

"Extremely unlikely. I will tell you this, and I'll stake my rep on it — if this ore was mined in Death Valley I'll eat it!"

Though he was shaking with anger, face poisonously blotched, the big man refused to let himself be persuaded. He wanted, was determined to believe Slim had found another mine. Experts had been wrong before. What a fool he would look if this smug bastard was right, buying Jenkens' notes, buying back his own ore, bandying words —

"This is high-grade, E.P.; some of the finest jewelry rock I have ever examined. Be reasonable, sir! He could have handpicked this stuff before he sold you the mine —"

"You call it reasonable to believe a deadbeat like Jenkens with his ass hanging out would sit for three years on a bagful of ore worth eight thousand dollars!"

The assayer, shrugging, got up and put on his hat. "You wanted my opinion; you paid for it. You got it."

"If he comes in with another load will you still try to tell me —"

"He won't." The assayer put on his infuriating smugness. "At least," he said, hedging, "not *this* kind of stuff. Conceivably he might pack in some more rock, but subtle differences will be discernible." The bland smile flashed out across his teeth. "To the practiced eye . . ."

But King Ezra waved him away, feeling better. Pin them down hard and fast and there wasn't one "expert" out of a hundred didn't jump to cover his pontifical pronouncements in a veritable forest of ifs and buts. Obviously Jenkens had found another mine. Whether it was or was not the same formation was of negligible significance when stood up against the magnitude of possible profits. The fool had made another strike, and the need that took hold of Carltenmore's attention was to batten down the hatches and made certain he got every ounce he had coming — and which he damned sure would. Yes, indeed!

There was another frowsy grasper on the edges of this deal, a man tied in with

Carltenmore, whose designs and lewd hallucinations had also been subjected, through Jenkens, to considerable wear and tear of late. Pheppy Titus was a handsome general superintendent of Mammoth Mines, Inc. and was considered among the sporting crowd to be something of a lady-killer. In his current pursuit of Dolores Ramirez, he appeared to be encountering an appalling lack of progress. He, too, had a standing to consider, and his patience with these frustrations was just about used up.

Accustomed to easy conquests, vain of his prowess and social accomplishments, Titus could not understand the girl's scornful repulsion. It intrigued and incensed him, whetting his appetite, haunting his dreams — a defiant challenge, imbuing the wench with the enchantments of Circe. The challenge of her disdainful repudiations was the kind of thing to drive a man wild — and that goddamn Jenkens!

Twice now that brush-popping clown had thrown him off and made him look a damn bungler right on the brink of almost certain success. He guessed he would have to take care of the feller; but it was the girl herself that had Pheppy chewing his toe-nails. Who in Noah's name did she think she was? The Van Asterbilt filly!

She had better come down off her high horse, and quick, if she didn't want her old man — and that tribe of kids — to wake up some morning right out on the street. It could damn well happen! And that miserable, worthless, bootlicking Elfego — what did he imagine all those privileges were for! On account of his cough?

Titus, swearing, caught up his hat and, sending round for his carriage, set off full of phlegm for the Casa Ramirez.

XII

While King Ezra was heating the trails up with couriers dispatched by the hour to find and fetch his pet sidewinder, the subject of all this commotion, H. C. Jenkens — celebrated in newsprint as the "Death Valley Midas" — was moving full steam ahead with his plans for making Carltenmore look the south end of a mighty sorry horse going north.

Although filled with the heady fragrance of revenge Slim was not unmindful of ever-present dangers. He kept a sharp eye about him and wherever he could he clung to the rimrocks, scanning every crevice, each suggestion of dust, with the bitter intensity of a hunted wolf. Out here he knew mighty well if he ran afoul of Hell Creek he would get no second chance.

Bumping into Charlie in town he could probably afford, but out here in the sagebrush where there was no one to see but the vinegarroons and gophers and Carltenmore's paid Injuns, the bloody bastard would kill him like a mad dog.

Twice Slim saw signal smokes and once

he even glimpsed a couple of Ezra's couriers tearing along like hell wouldn't have them. He went into a fine sweat, mistaking these for a pair of Charlie's gore-hungry scouts. He crouched in his tracks never moving a muscle for a good ten minutes after the riders disappeared before he could get up enough spit to cuss with, vindictively adding this to Carltenmore's bill.

It took him three full days, anti-godlin around the way he'd been doing, to raise sight of town. Bellied down on a hilltop, studying the view through the vantage of a battered Army telescope, he decided he would better hold off until morning. He wanted plenty of light and people abroad when he took these mulepacks of rock into Goldfield to flaunt them under King Ezra's nose.

It was nine o'clock and turning hot in the sun when Slim passed the Anaconda Mill with his mules and cut west over South to swing into Second before pointing them north toward the heart of town. Traffic was lighter here than on Main. There wasn't much wheeled stuff using this route, there was less dust to cope with and not so much bustle, only a few businesses with plenty of open spaces a man could take off through should imminent prospects indicate such a need.

All went well until he got pretty near to Myers, one block south of Crook and Diall's livery. There, as he approached the intersection, still walking in the thought that should there happen to be any occasion for gunplay he might have more chance if he was out of the saddle, a horseless carriage — spluttering loudly on too lean a spark — came wheeling south out of Crook, the sun winking mirror-like flashes from the gleaming brass of its hand-buffed lamps. If this had not been enough, streamers of cloth, flapping like pant's legs, trailed from both sides of the square-set windscreen.

Forward went Gretchen's ears like fixed bayonets. Backing up against Slim she half lifted a hoof; then, taking comfort from his unflustered presence, she rolled her eyes disdainfully. But Zachary Taylor, the big brainless lummox, let out a wild snort and, extending himself, took off for the tules, squeaking like he was made out of fresh-cut goose quills.

Powerful expletives burst from Slim's throat, terms of opprobrium so sulfurous and sizzling you wondered they didn't go straight up in smoke. Glomming into the saddle he flung Gretchen round and, glowering into the dust of Zach's precipitate departure, raked her sides with the bang of his spurs.

That she-mule really heated her axles. She got down to business in the first three jumps, put so much of herself so whole-heartedly into it that before Zach had gone two blocks they were up with him, lapped on him, Jenkens' unrestrained language blistering the air to the grinning delight of several half naked youngsters peering out of a dooryard through a nearly-down fence.

"Gee, mister! Gee!" one yelled. "Do it again — huh?"

Zach stood wide-eyed, nervously trembling. Jenkens, face gone tight as granite, came out of his saddle like the wrath of God. He grabbed Zach's halter, shook out the shank; and then, making ready to learn him a lesson, saw the heads sticking out of doors and windows. Mouth shut like the jaws of a trap he stabbed a look at the load, freshened his grip on the rope and struck out at right angles, hauling the silenced mule toward the road.

The word had spread. People came running from every direction, jostling and pawing and ringing him in, shouting questions, some booing, others begging for samples till, angered, he reached up and covered both ears.

They all knew him now. They'd seen his name in the papers. They pushed and they pulled and their clamor rose louder for here, in the flesh, was the Death Valley Slim of the stories, the man whose Midas-like touch had reopened the mines, restored the camp's faith, sent its good stocks and bad soaring upward like eagles. Some of his luck was bound to rub off if only they could get themselves close enough to him.

But when they started to reach for the packs on his mules Jenkens came out of himself with a curse. "You crazy dang wallopers!" he snarled lividly, "Git back!" and snatched out his pistol; but of course he was fooling. Old Death Valley Slim would haul the shirt off his back if he thought by so doing it would make some nump happy; and they crowded in closer, tugging at the knots that held his ore sacks in place.

Desperate, Slim began to empty his pockets. He still had some of the gold pieces left he had traded Reilly out of and that scribbling bird, Featherstone. He cast them about him like pearls before swine, and while they were scrambling and snatching he shoved his mules through and regained the street.

He felt like he'd been caught up in a twister, but the way was clear now and, forgetting all about the chastisement of Zach, he herded his charges for Diall's on the double; and was about to turn in and put their care on the livery when he happened to remember the last time he'd been there. Laugh at him, would they! Play poormouth and hound him for debts the Great Seizer had already bought up! Hell with him — with all of 'em! And he chased the protesting mules on past.

An old man came running from the place, wildly waving. "Jenkens! Hey, Jenkens! Ye're puttin' up here, ain't ye? Got ye down fer them two biggest stalls, we hev — got a cot all set up in the office an' . . ."

Slim stopped to look back. "Well ain't that just ducky! You musta been lunchin' on loco," he hooted, "or was it them lies you seen in the papers?"

"I — We —" The man looked to be twisting in a convulsion of anguish. "It was just . . ." His eyes darted past to peer again at Slim's packs, and you'd have thought from his tone he was about to break down and bawl. "Slim, boy," he groaned, "ain't

122

we always been your friends at this stable?"

But Slim's stare turned hard. "It's the 'friends' in this world a man's got to watch out for!"

The codger's face got red and then it turned yeasty, but the look of those packs was a powerful reminder of Jenkens' changed status. Zach was starting to edge back. His master picked up a rock. The hostler said with reproach, "A man ought to stand with them that sticks by him. Who stood by you when ye didna hev a pot? All them bills ye run up —"

"Yeah!" Jenkens snarled, remembering the way they'd sold him out to King Ezra. "If you'd hung onto them notes you'd be on Easy Street now instead of pickin' up fifty cents on the dollar."

"Forty-three, Slim."

"That's the way she rolls," Slim said with a grin. "A man can't afford to be friends with a bum." And, dropping the rock, he hiked after his mules.

XIII

It came over him, tramping after them, he'd likely be a heap smarter holing up with Elfego, it being the habit of lightning never to follow the same track twice. It wasn't just Tomas that kept him away, and the girl *had* been nice — mighty helpful, in fact; but there was things worse than lightning a man had to reckon with. He could have put up with Tomas — even Tomas *and* the girl, except that over every female — knock-kneed, bug-eyed, fat or frail — was the ever-swinging noose of double harness, and Dolores had made her intentions plain. So he choused the mules east a-ways into Main and then, hanging hard to Zach's halter shank, lugged them north through the traffic past both banks and theaters, attracting little attention but plenty of curses, to bring up finally in front of the hotel.

He wasn't too worried at the moment about Charlie, but he was considerably disconcerted when the burly doorman flatly refused either to let the mules in or to stand out there hanging onto them for him.

A crowd was hurriedly coming together and in the midst of the altercation Jenkens, very much aware of this and of the grins, declaimed loudly, "Right! Who's talkin' about right?" His face got red and, waving his arms, he became even more noisily obnoxious. "I guess," he said, "you think it's *right* I should spend all my time stumblin' around in the heat of Death Valley fryin' my brains out huntin' up mines for that overstuffed hog Ezra P. Carltenmore! Him that sits all day on a cushioned sofa cooled by fans in his palatial office, pullin' strings an' pushin' buttons, handin' out orders like he was Pharaoh of Egypt! That's right, huh?

"Well, what about *me!* That's what *I* wanta know! You think it's right I should work my fingers to the bone for a pat on the head or a kick in the pants if I don't pile the moola up fast enough fer 'im? How would *you* like t' be hunted an' hounded from piller t' post by a bushwhackin' killer an' a bunch of red Injuns sicced on by a skunk that's got so big on the sweat an' the blood an' the golrammed bones of the dumb clunk miners an' prospectors he's skinned, the law ain't even about t' go after him! An' why, you ask? I'll tell you why! Because of bribes an' influ-

125

ence an' accepted favors, the dogs you people have put into office git the shakes just imaginin' tryin' t' bark back at him!"

"A pack of lies!" a voice snapped harshly, and the outraged face of Mr. Pheppy Titus, general superintendent of the Carltenmore enterprises, began to move up through the twisting heads. People quickly fell back to give the room that was the rightful due of so important a gentleman, and Slim's lip curled in disgust.

"That's right," he sneered, looking scathingly around, "bend your necks — git 'em down. Why'n't you lick his boots while you're at it! Ain't he the Number Two puke fer King Ezra? Get down there an' grovel, you mealymouthed chumps! Show the big —"

"Have a care," Titus said but, with his temper well reined and apparently in hand. "That kind of talk is actionable, Jenkens, and if you don't want to find yourself behind bars —"

"Go ahead, intimidate me. Give 'em a sample of the way you sports operate."

"Keep talking," Titus smiled.

"You bet I'll keep talkin'!"

"All right. You've been warned."

"That figures," said Slim. "First the threat, then the warnin'. After that, if the guy ain't been clubbed by some of yer bully boys, the rack an' the dungeons, or mebbe a visit from Hell Creek Charlie."

Titus reared back. "There are laws —"

"An' pet judges an' bought-off juries an' witnesses hauled outa dives an' deadfalls an' all the rest of the claptrap you privileged bastards throw around with yer weight. Don't tell me! I've *been* there, mister. Tell the rest of these yaps what don't know no better. How the laws is doped t' keep the poor on their treadmills an' make the rich richer! Laws that give license t' nabobs like you to hound miners' daughters —"

"Now see here!" Titus blustered, beginning to look sick; but Slim, who had just spied Featherstone and several of his scribbling colleagues in the crowd, all putting it down fast as fingers could fly, yelled, "I know what I seen! You an' that stope boss haulin' that Ramirez kid out of her saddle. If I hadn't come by no tellin' what devilment you'd of been up to, a scoundrel with no more conscience than *you* got! You oughta be run outa town on a rail."

But Pheppy had already run, slunk away — gone like the dew in the noonday sun. The crowd, turned restive, was scowling and muttering. Scoop Featherstone, trailed by other pad-clutching gentry, pushed through the mob to gain additional tidbits. Slim, vociferously indignant, declared he didn't know which was the worst, a cad like Carltenmore's general superintendent preying on young girls and new-made widders or polecats like King Ezra himself, fattening on the sweat of underpaid miners and the usurious profits wrung from dang fools caught up in the toils of his prospector's contract.

A simple man, standing there in his rags, speaking out for the masses, speaking straight from the heart. It was downright impressing; and the newshounds, caring only for headlines, let the crowd lap it up. Then the man from the *Wall Street Journal* cut in. "Are we to understand, Mister Jenkens, Carltenmore's grubstake agreement with you has expired?"

"It run plumb out," Jenkens growled, "three months ago." He got it out of his jeans and passed it to Scoop who let the other reporters read it over his shoulder. A man repping for one of the other big dailies wanted to know if he could print it. "Help yourself," said Slim magnanimously; but the *Journal*'s man wasn't satisfied yet. "I understand from Mister Carltenmore he advanced you in excess of fifteen hundred dollars. Is that correct?"

"He never give me more'n ten dollars at one time. Mostly he give me fives. He never give *me* a nickel! Not personal. He done all his business direct with the outfitters."

"But over the whole period of the contract —"

"The contract's expired!" Slim glared, bristling. "Whose side are you on here, anyway?"

The *Journal's* correspondent considered him unreadably. "But you'll admit it's possible —"

"I ain't admittin' a golrammed thing! The facts of this business is open an' shut. The guy's been out t' do me in, just like he done on that deal for the Mammoth — fixin' t' leave me out in the cold! When it come over him I mighta hit again he drags out that grubstake agreement, figurin' t' come down on me fer half. When that didn't wash he drags out a pocketful of notes he's bought up an' threatens to tie me up in the courts!"

"He could certainly sue —"

"Well, let him," said Jenkens, and showed a crafty grin. "Lawin' an' gittin' ain't quite the same thing."

"He'll get a judgement," Featherstone said.

"On what?"

"On this mine you've just found —"

"I ain't located no mine."

The Wall Street man said patiently, "He'll find it."

Slim said with a snort, "He'll play hell, too! How you goin' t' find somethin' that never has been?" And he laughed at their looks, loudly whacking his thigh.

Featherstone said, "That ore you brought in —"

"That was stole," Jenkens laughed. "I fetched a bigger batch this time. Must be close t' twenty grand on Gretchen there an' Zachary Taylor — them mules," he explained, taking in the bugged eyes. "An' every chunk of it better'n the last."

The *Journal*'s man looked around, shook his head. "I can't find," he said, "checking back on you, that even those you've mooched on the worst have ever suggested you might pick up things that didn't belong to you." He lit up a stogie, eying Slim through the smoke.

"I should hope not," Slim said. Then he reached out and tapped the reporter on the chest. "Did I say *I* stole it? You better clean out your ears." He turned to the mules and suddenly whipped out his pistol. "Git away from them packs!"

The pair of pilfering townsmen jumped back in a hurry. "Hell," one said, "we was jest huntin' souvenirs," and the other guy said, "You was flingin' 'em around free enough on that last trip —"

"That was then. This is now," Jenkens growled, scowling fierce. And while he was doing it a man came up and whispered into his ear. Slim's eyes winnowed down, then he grunted an affirmative. He caught up Zach's halter shank. Putting his shooter away he stepped into the saddle and, reining Gretchen around, forced the crowd to back off.

"What's up?" Scoop called, peering like he sniffed news, but Jenkens brushed him aside.

He said, like Moses handing down the twelve stones, "From here on out I play like the rest of the toughs around here. Go write that in yer papers. *Typhoon fashion!* Now git outa my way!"

XIV

The whispering jasper was about out of sight, the flap of his breeze-stretched coat tails even now disappearing around the building's far corner — not that Slim gave a whoop. He knew where to go and he knew how to get there. But just as he was about to bang Gretchen with the spurs he looked back at Scoop carefully, and somewhat hesitantly said, "What ever come of that funny lookin' ore them Sandstorm leasers chucked out on the dump?"

Featherstone wasn't in too good a mood, still graveled maybe over the arrogant way Slim had give him the brush-off. But he was too good a newshawk to let personal feelings scuff up his approach to what just might turn out to be the story of the year. Ironing the scowl off his face, he said, "The new guys, soon as they had the dope on it, picked all that up and shipped it off at huge profit."

"It was all right, then?"

Featherstone laughed. "Turned out, by the ton, to be about the richest ore the mines in this area have produced — up to now, at least."

He put his steno book away, the slanch of his stare taking on a thoughtful shine. The crowd, now that Slim appeared about to take off, was breaking up, fixing to go its several ways, resolving into garrulous groups of threes and fours, while some of its components with no immediate acquaintances in sight straggled off by themselves to hunt scenes more rewarding. Scoop's glance juned around. Most of his colleagues had gone. Lowering his voice he leaned nearer. "What did that feller want?"

Slim's grin was cagey.

After a moment Scoop said, "We had a deal, remember?"

Slim looked down at himself. He guessed he looked pretty frowsy. His boots were so frazzled he could hardly scratch a match without burning his feet. "I gotta git me some glad rags. I got to find me a room —"

"If you're going to play nob you should recruit the talents of a man who's at home in the flossiest circles," Scoop said, "meaning me. Tycoons don't patronize the ready-made racks or put up in flea traps. To shine in their company a man's got to have class. Put yourself in my hands and —"

"Hoo hoo!" Jenkens snorted, but it was

plain he was tempted.

Scoop said, "All I want is the inside track. I don't care about your mine, and I sure ain't after your money. Just give me first chance to get my stuff on the wires and you'll be on the front pages of the nation's biggest dailies. We'll make Carltenmore look so sick —"

"It's a deal," Slim said, and stuck out his hand.

Scoop, pumping it, said, "Now what about that guy?"

"What guy?" Jenkens' eyes opened wide.

Featherstone grabbed a deep breath and hung onto it. Mouth shut tight he started off, Slim glaring after him. When it became evident he was sure enough leaving, Slim glared even harder. "Fer cripes sake," he grumbled. "It was just a few words from that friend of yours, Reilly."

With one leg off the ground Scoop's face came around. Slim grudgingly said, "Critter loaded me up with some stock he wants back."

Featherstone, staring, finally put down his foot. "What you need is a goddamn wet nurse." He looked, by grab, like Slim didn't have enough sense to pound sand. "I suppose you were figuring to hand it right over!"

Jenkens' cheeks fired up. "You don't even know what I'm talkin' about. Anyway," he declared, "I was goin' over first t' see how much the First National would give." Then he said, sounding riled, "I ain't a complete fool!"

"Well, that's news," Scoop sniffed. "How many shares of that stuff have you got?"

"I've got a few hundred."

"Of course," the reporter sighed, "it's just coincidence the Sullivan Trust, which is George Graham Rice, is about three thousand short of what they've sold, and that Reilly happens to be one of Rice's runners." He eyed Slim scathingly. "Give me that bundle and I'll see what I can —"

"Oh, no you don't!" Jenkens growled, backing Gretchen away.

Scoop threw up his hands. "All right. Play it your way. But at least take time to spruce up a little; see John Crook before you make any deals — and don't buy your clothes from some damn outfitter. Go to a tailor; try Franz Petz. And get yourself a suite at the Goldfield Hotel."

"All right, gran'maw," Slim said meekly. "Anythin' else, before I go, you wanta say?"

"Sure you don't want me to go with you?" And then Scoop added, not without malice, "Most of these typhoons, you know, employ a few fellers to look after their interests."

Slim, thinking he meant gun handlers, paled a little, being reminded of Charlie, that just about now was probably fit to be tied. But, squaring his jaw, Jenkens shook his head. "Don't you worry about me."

"Very well. I'll see you at dinner," Scoop said, buttoning his coat up against the wind. "Remember now, see John Crook, Crook & Company bank, across from the First National. And," he said, grinning, "let somebody else do part of the talking."

Jenkens, scowling after him, thought, *He ain't so dang smart!* Then he turned his mules and headed for Petz's place over on Ramsey. Before he'd gone very far it occurred to him that a really big mogul — say a nabob like Ezra — wouldn't go to no tailor. "He'd call the tailor to him," he told the mules; and Gretchen, at least, was in full agreement. So he hauled them around and pretty soon was trekking east on Crook, heading for the hotel which was on Columbia just south of the post office.

He got five rooms, with butler service, had a meal sent up, left a call for the barber and sent off the butler to round up Franz Petz. It took a deal of persuasion and considerable moola but, by dint of much yelling and some unprintable language, Slim had his new clothes in time for dinner.

After dinner, Slim spent the next hour in the hotel lobby — arguing stock prices and dealin' with men from Sullivan Trust and Crook and Company. Crook wouldn't come anywhere near Rice's offer, so he returned to his room.

He was there but a few minutes when someone knocked on the corridor door.

He sent Cyril to answer it. Scoop was let in. His eyes took in Slim from new Justins to Stetson.

"You look," he said, "like the canary just after he swallowed the cat."

"It was your idea. What's the matter with these rags — ain't they glad enough fer you?"

"That lavender waistcoat . . ." Scoop shook his head. "Did you see Crook?"

"They won't come inside shootin' distance of what Rice offered."

"The point," Scoop said, "is they'll do what they say they will."

But Slim, firing up a fifty-cent cheroot, continued to look pretty pleased with himself. "An' you think Rice won't? Hell, you said yourself he has t' git them shares —"

"He has to get what he's short; he don't have to get them from you."

"Where else could he pick up that many in a hurry? You oughta heard him. He wanted to come right up —"

"What'd you tell him?"

"Said I'd think about it. He might even come up some."

"He might promise you the moon, but that doesn't mean you'll get it." Scoop said dryly, "Given a choice, a man who'll —"

"What are you howlin' about?" Slim wanted to know. "You'll git your story whichever way she squirts." He looked resentfully down his long nose. "Trouble with you is you think no one else has got anythin' under his hat but hair." He jerked the bell-cord for Cyril. "Have 'em send up two dinners an' a bucket of champagne — an' tell 'em I want the best in the house!"

"What are you going to do with that ore you brought in?" the reporter asked presently.

"Been figurin' I'd sell it to the Anaconda people. You got any objections?"

Scoop, leaning back, arms behind head on the horsehair sofa, considered Slim through half-shut eyes. "Nope," he said, "it's your neck and your money. I've said all I'm going to."

"Well, bully fer you!" Slim cried delightedly. "Now we got the basis fer a first-class arrangement. You write the stories an' I'll dish up the dirt."

If Featherstone's look was skeptical, at least he kept his reservations to himself. They enjoyed a good meal and after they were finished the reporter, pleading other work, took his departure. But, as Cyril let him out of the suite, he could not resist one final question. "When," he said, "are you going after Ezra?"

Jenkens chuckled. "It's his move, ain't it?"

"You told the boys this morning you stole that ore. Suppose he claims you stole it from him?"

Jenkens' face was bland with guile. "He wouldn't do that. Hell, he's cock of the walk — even if he thought he could make it stick he wouldn't want that kinda guff makin' the rounds. Besides, he'd never believe it. He's too much like you; thinks he's got all the brains in Nevada," Slim grinned. "He'd sooner chop off both legs an' then his right arm than admit he got took by the likes of me. An' don't worry about that ore. I've got it locked up in the hotel safe."

Yes, sir! Slim figured he was sitting in the driver's seat now. This whole deal was coming off slicker than slobbers. Things was moving his way. Hell Creek and them scouts was still prowling Death Valley. King Ezra by now was bound to know Slim was back with two more muleloads of gold. When he got his slip from the mill and made it public — this was far richer rock than he had fetched in before — that old bullshovin' hypothecator would start jumping around like a scorpion had crawled up his pant's leg.

After finishing off what was left of the champagne Slim, feeling the urge to spread himself a little, decided he might as well go over and trade Rice his stock and, on the way back, maybe drop by the livery and flash his roll for a few belly laughs.

It was crowding ten when Slim stepped into the Sullivan Trust, which was open, brightly lighted and, apparently, doing a considerable business. Hardly had Jenkens got inside the doors than Shanghai Larry, widely smiling a welcome, came up in best Sunday collar and hames. This charm did not fade when he caught Slim's name, but his voice kind of wheezed like maybe he'd got a frog in his swallower. Saying he guessed this was more in Rice's department he scuttled off to jerk open a frosted-glass door.

Rice came straight along. "Mister Jenkens, how are you?" He got hold of Slim's hand. "Real pleasure, I'm sure. Ah, perhaps we'd better go into my office. Did you bring those shares?"

"Yep," Slim grinned after G. G. Rice had shut the door. "All twenty-four hundred and eighty-seven of 'em."

Rice's brows drew down. "I thought you said *two* hundred —"

"You thought wrong."

"I don't know. . . ."

Slim got up. "Make up yer mind. There's other fish waitin' —"

"Oh, I'll take them," Rice said. He waved Slim toward a chair and reached for his desk. "I'll have one of the clerks fix up a draft —"

"No drafts," Slim grinned. Their eyes met and fastened. "Thousan' dollar bills. That's my speed," said the man from Death Valley.

Across the desk Rice stared. "Makes no difference to us, but do you feel that's wise? Two hundred and forty-eight. You got somebody waiting?"

Jenkens scoffed. "You worry about you. I'll take care of *me!*"

"Pretty risky," Rice said; and then, with a shrug, plopped his hand on a button. To the man who came in he said casually, "Bring me two hundred and forty-eight thousand-dollar bills."

He glanced back at Jenkens. "Do you have the shares with you?"

"Twenty-four hundred an' eighty-seven Sandstorms comin' right up," Slim grinned, and pushed them over.

Rice leafed through them, cool as a cucumber. "You'll have to endorse these." He moved a bottle of ink and a pen nearer Slim and then sat back to enjoy his smoke. While Slim was inking the papers the feller came back with a bundle of bank notes an inch and a half thick. Rice, still smoking, counted them into Slim's hands.

Jenkens stood up, feeling seven feet tall. "Thanks for the profit."

"Any time," Rice smiled. "Sure you wouldn't like for me to send someone with you?"

Jenkens scowled. "What do you think I pack this rod fer?" and dug the big pistol out of his waistband. Twirling it a couple of times by the trigger guard he dropped it into a pocket of his coat. "Bring down a catamount at forty paces."

"Guess it would, at that." Rice walked to the door with him. "Well, keep your powder dry." He passed Slim through and closed the door.

With his roll in one pocket, his gun in the other and a hand around each, Jenkens moved off the stoop and went flat on his face.

XV

The part of the program devoted to pyrotechnics was among the most colorful Slim could remember; rare new setpieces were displayed at both sides while the main attraction, directly overhead, appeared to consist of shooting stars in a variety of colors not generally seen — blue and orange and lavender and pink, while the roar of the crowd rose like a high wind. He seemed, filled with a kind of breathless wonder, almost to be soaring among them himself, to be in suspension, sort of floating in circles with his feet hanging over his head.

Somewhere, in that awful dark, a clap like a thunderbolt shook him loose. Now he was plummeting like a shot eagle, the wind screaming round him with the screech of trussed pigs; and in an agony of terror he saw the great rocks, the crags of bald mountains, reared up one upon another, all hungrily waiting the moment of impact. He felt his flesh going through them like the tines of a fork through new cut hay. All motion stopped. A firm yet resilient warmth seemed to couch him.

With a fearful groan he jerked open both eyes.

Twin peaks loomed above him, horizontally thrust from an indeterminate field which may have been mist but looked more like deep snow. Then they moved, dipped, hung trembling just above Slim's wild stare. A hand appeared. Sound returned in a jabber of questions. The couch moved beneath him and a girl's anxious voice over and over was whispering his name. His glance swept out across the forest of legs, the goggling faces. His horrified brain began sluggishly to tell him he was flat on his back with his head in the lap of Dolores Ramirez.

He sprang up with a curse, all wabbly and shaking, pawing at the pocket in which he'd cached his big roll. The pocket was flat, limp as King Ezra's handshake, and he knew in a flash he'd been struck down and robbed.

Filled with bitterness and confusion, he had his mouth all puckered to give vent to his rage when his eyes, raking over those avid faces winnowed to crafty slits as he grasped how he'd look if he should blurt out the truth. Hoist with his own petard, in all conscience as big a fool as he'd been scheming to make King Ezra seem.

He bent to brush the dirt off his clothes, inwardly seething, railing at the scurviness of his jezebel luck — or, he thought, furious — *was* this just luck? Filled with the tumult of his burgeoning suspicions he looked around again, finding Rice's concerned features sandwiched in between the faces of Pheppy Titus and his pet stope boss with, just back of them the interested stares of Scoop Featherstone and Jimmy O'Brien of the Goldfield *News*.

"What happened?" O'Brien called, shoving forward with pad and pencil. And Scoop, with his own tools was right at his heels.

Slim, about then, would have suspected his own grandmother, but he could see they had him over a barrel. He hadn't one shred of the flimsiest evidence. If he squawked they would make him out a plumb fool!

Feeling more like a draggle-winged sparrow than the camp's newest nabob, Henry Clay Jenkens, chewing hard on his lip, peered around for Dolores, wanting to hear what she might contribute; for if the girl had discovered him — if it was she whose screams had fetched the others, she might have seen something. But Elfego's daughter had slipped away.

"Musta been somethin' I et," Slim growled. "Got a little dizzy — guess I musta blacked out." He felt the breath drop out of his words, blackly staring at the shape of Carltenmore's hat coming toward him through the shift of bodies opening up to make a path.

"Well, well!" said the great man, teetering on boot heels while his cold stare skewered the roundabout faces. "I was told you were back. And, as usual, I see, you've managed to drum up a crowd. Still throwing away those counterfeit gold pieces?"

"As a matter of fact," Slim said with a grin, "I dropped by to get rid of some Sandstorm stock. Got a tip the bottom was about to fall out again. You know how it is with these speculative properties . . . like Mammoth. Up today and down tomorrer. What with Rice here sellin' 'em short, an' all, it struck me I better git into somethin' solid. Which I done," he chuckled, rearing back with his chin up in a take-off on Ezra.

Some of the crowd sniggered, for Carltenmore had not endeared himself to everyone. But others appeared rather darkly thoughtful, stabbing covert glances between the two men as though fearful such talk might be the harbinger of disaster. Indeed, several of their number —

and, strangely enough, these would seem the most affluent — somewhat precipitantly departed. One might almost have sensed in their darting looks the mounting panic of nervous shareholders.

Slim, watching all this, had himself a good laugh.

The Grubstake King appeared about as bowed up as a feller could get and still stay on the ground. His left eye twitched and the mountainous rest of him quivered and jerked like a cat on a tin roof.

This man, this victim of his own power and greed — of a mind that could not bear to be thwarted — seemed more to be pitied than censored just now. A giant of the times, one of the pillars of rapacity, he was a Goliath of the town's expanding economy. To be so bearded and mocked by such a gadfly as Slim must have seemed a kind of a blasphemy. And there is always about the collapse of the mighty something sad and nostalgic, as in the passing of an era. The familiar, no matter how objectionable, is weirdly preferred to the untried, the unknown.

Jenkens felt the fishy stares, the crowd's resentful apprehension. But the cracks in Carltenmore's armor were the things he must find and some how expose if ever he would get the best of the feller. One weakness, at least, was beginning to show in the poisonous bloating of that furious face.

So Slim, in the bind of his own gnawing setback, did what he could to goad Carltenmore into overplaying his hand. "When're you goin' t' open up that mine an' give them Bohunks a chance to eat again? What's the matter with the Mammoth?" he jeered, with his eyes rolled back like he'd got onto something special. "I coulda told you that vein was due t' pinch out," and he laughed again at the man's livid look.

"There is nothing whatever the matter with that vein!" the big man declared when he could trust himself to speak. But the fury that was in him made it come out too loud. Now some of those most closely tied in with him began to stir uneasily. There were dubious mutterings. Even the elegant Pheppy Titus, who had ought to know the truth of it if anyone did, began to throw speculative glances his way. None of which the king missed.

He made a visible effort to get hold of himself, but before he could make any further pronouncements Jenkens said with a sneer, "If there's nothin' the matter with it why's the mine closed? I'll say one thing —

if you don't git it open pretty dang quick you won't have a bootstrapper left in this camp." And he looked at the crowd, flexing his jaws in a grin.

"I'll open it," Carltenmore shouted, "when I'm damn good and ready!"

"If it would help you t' *git* ready, to mebbe get up a shipment," Slim grinned, "I could let you have some of that rock. Say!" he exclaimed, like it surprised even himself, "is that why you bought up all that last sack I fetched? Hell, what'll you give fer some really *good* ore?"

Carltenmore's cheeks were the color of apoplexy. Jenkens' insinuations would not put the Mammoth into *borrasca* except maybe in the minds of a bunch of damned fools, but this was something Ezra couldn't afford. The Mammoth was incorporated. Its stock was vulnerable. Jenkens' innuendos could undermine confidence and drive Mammoth's shares down to give-away prices. It was probably what that devil was up to.

Clawing his collar the Grubstake King, beholding the expressions twisting some of those faces, was driven into attempting to defend his position. Harried into speech, trying to shift blame while caught off balance and so black-cat mad he was goaded onto ground not thoroughly examined, the flustered tycoon cried, "We wouldn't *be* closed if it wasn't for you and your . . ."

"Me!" Jenkens hooted. "You gone off your rocker?"

"You've disrupted our whole operation —"

"I ain't even been *near* your dabratted mine!"

"Is that so?" The king sneered. "You may find yourself telling that to the judge. My assayer, Blackey Dawson, is convinced this ore you've been packing around came out of the Mammoth! And what do you think about that?" he yelled, frothing.

"I think, by grab, you got a hole in yer head. You'll never salt it with some of the stuff *I've* fetched in! I think you've cooked up a deal with that sonofabitch — but take it into the courts if you wanta git laughed clean outa the country! You've had the shaft closed up tight and armed guards so thick it's a wonder, by cripes, they ain't half of 'em been trampled — a goddamn fly couldn't git into them stopes! You go right ahead if you're that big a chump."

Carltenmore said, half strangled, "All I have to prove is it's Mammoth ore! I can impound that rock you just brought in —"

"Go ahead," Jenkens grinned. "Grab my

mules while you're at it, an' the clothes off my back. Have yourself a real time. An' when you can't make it stick I'll have the Mammoth back, too, along with all the rest of the loot you've finagled — if the lawyers don't clean you out plumb naked first!"

XVI

Slim felt so good when he woke up the next morning he dawdled in bed until pretty near ten, remembering and chuckling at how blustery and foolish he had made Ezra look, and at the daubs he had put on the Carltenmore image. By now the word would be all over town. Wrapped in this heady glow he could even make light of the loss of his Sandstorm profits. It was found money anyhow; and when he sold the ore in the hotel safe he would have all he needed for the purposes in hand.

Pulling on his boots he had the bellboy take his breakfast order, and had another good belly laugh while Cyril was running the water for his shave. Back of his ear, where that feller had slugged him when he'd stepped from the Sullivan Trust last night, a lump had come out about the size of a goose egg, but the skin wasn't broke and he guessed, thinking of Ezra, he could make out to stand it. He even considered dropping around to see Dolores, a warming good-Samaritan thought he had no intention of developing further.

The boy came with the cart and helped Cyril lay the table, and Jenkens magnanimously flipped him a gold piece, waving away his stammered thanks. In this happy mood he got on with his breakfast until his man obsequiously laid beside his plate a folded edition of the Goldfield *News*.

A scare head ran clear across the front page. JENKENS STRUCK DOWN BY UNKNOWN ASSAILANT. Shaking like he was in a high wind, Jenkens' eyes dug out the gist of the story. It carried the by-line of Jimmy O'Brien, who had certainly been at the scene last night, yet no mention was made of Carltenmore at all. It said H. C. Jenkens, the prospector known as Death Valley Slim, who had traded a sackful of samples for some Sandstorm shares shortly after the former leasers had sold out and departed, had stepped into the Sullivan Trust yesterday evening and sold those shares for two hundred and forty-eight thousand dollars; that he had subsequently been struck down in the street and relieved of the money, which was in currency. Jenkens, it continued, had been found, still unconscious, by Dolores Ramirez, a miner's daughter, some minutes later. In one of the victim's pants' pockets there were six double eagles. The police, in view of this evidence, considered the slugging to be the work of someone with advance information on Jenkens' business at the bank, the article concluded.

Slim pitched away the paper with a snarl. Only Featherstone had known he'd intended selling. Well, Cyril had heard him talking in the lobby and Rice, of course, may have discussed the conversation with some of his associates. But nobody else had known a thing, and he hadn't told one dang soul he'd been robbed! He sure as shooting hadn't talked to no cops!

Sloshing on his hat, Slim took off on the double with blood in his eye. He felt sure-enough pretty put out about it. He didn't put it past Rice to have engineered the whole deal — or Scoop Featherstone, either! The money was gone. He didn't care about that, but he was sure going to make a believer of somebody!

He stepped out in the lobby still foaming and fuming, but partway to the doors he got a hail from the desk.

"Mister Jenkens!" The manager came trotting up, breathing hard, with his eyes looking like two holes burnt in a bed sheet. "I . . . you — I'm afraid you're not going to like this, but —"

"Later!" Jenkens growled and, cutting

round the man, rushed into the street where he flagged a hack and had himself carried to the Goldfield *News*. Storming into the place he loudly demanded an audience with the editor. "An' right damn *now* if you don't want this rag sued!"

"Well," O'Brien grinned, coming out to the counter, "how's the head this morning? What's the news from Death Valley? Have they caught that —"

Slim's hand cut down in an irascible sweep. "I want a full retraction of that story you printed —"

"Just a minute," O'Brien said, beckoning up a couple of men behind the rail, each of whom promptly dug out pad and pencil. "What was the matter with it?"

"What's the idea of them?" Slim scowled, eyes bright with suspicion.

"The business of this newspaper is news," its proprietor said, quite unruffled. "If you wish to say something for publication, go ahead. If it's important enough we'll try to make room —"

"You know damn well I didn't come here fer that!"

"All right. What's your beef?"

Slim, still glaring, chewed at his lip. But he calmed down considerable, something about the air in this place suggesting if he

156

didn't step careful he might be in over his ears. Deciding to approach the matter a bit more obliquely he said with a lot less heat in his voice, "Who give you that dope on what the cops thought?"

O'Brien said, smiling, "It came straight from the Chief."

"I never seen no cops — they never ast me a thing."

"They have their ways. You didn't lodge a complaint?"

"I can wipe my *own* nose, an' you better believe it. How'd you know I sold that stock? How'd you know what I got? Or that I'd been robbed, or what was left in my pockets?"

"Miss Ramirez told us about those gold pieces. The rest of our information comes under the head of "privileged communication." Our informant requested his name be with—"

"Then who's to say he didn't make the whole thing right up out of his head?"

"If you want to say so," O'Brien grinned, "we'll print it. The sale of the stock is a matter of record." His grin widened out. "Is there anything else you'd want us to print?"

No one had to tell Slim he was wasting his time. Shutting his mouth hard enough to bust his choppers he flung about and stomped out, slamming the door mad enough to make it rattle.

"Perhaps," O'Brien called, opening it behind him, "you'd be interested in this," and he held out a proof on yellow paper.

Jenkens, suspicious, patently uneasy, walked back to the man and stood with his bristles up, glowering. "Hell, take it, man. It's not going to bite you," O'Brien said, snorting.

Accepting the galley, Slim dropped his glance to the boxed double column. It was a stop-press item without any by-line, and the print slammed into him like a hoof in the gut. He would sooner have been bitten.

Headed ORE IMPOUNDED the item went on to say that early that morning the police had entered the Goldfield Hotel, summoned the management and seized three sacks of ore from the hotel safe. The jewelry rock conservatively valued at over $100,000 and alleged to be the property of one Henry Clay Jenkens — more familiarly known as the Death Valley Midas — was impounded by officers on a complaint signed by the noted mining tycoon and Goldfield philanthropist Ezra P. Carltenmore, president of Mammoth Mines, Inc. to satisfy a judgement handed down against Jenkens in the matter of some notes taken up from local merchants who, apparently, had been unable to collect.

Following a paragraph of speculation concerning the source of Jenkens' mysterious bonanza, he was quoted as having declared it was "stole" and that he had no mine, that those seeing fit to question this statement were invited to go out and locate it if they could. "As we go to press," the article concluded, "reporters from this paper have been unable to contact Jenkens for comment."

It was a terrible blow. Slim was stunned, unable to think or — for the moment — even to break into one of his tirades, so cruel and unexpected was this latest buffeting at the hands of Ezra P. To be stripped of so much last night, and now this, was pretty near more than a plain single-blanket jackass prospector — even one so stout as the inimitable Jenkens — could be expected to stand up under. Then his eyes, turned hard, began to fill with hate. The skut expected this result. Paralyze and crush them — it was Carltenmore's answer to all who opposed him; and, if that didn't swamp 'em, there was always his hatchet man, Hell Creek Charlie. And now Slim's rage reared up so wild it pretty near choked him.

He didn't know quite how but, by grab, he'd show 'em! No whoppy-jawed this-an'-that son of a she-pig was going to wax fat on the sweat of *his* brow! Not by a danged sight!

He got back in his hack, still ranting and cursing, and when they climbed the final slope up from Main to pull around with a clatter before the sumptuous elegance of the Goldfield Hotel, he sprang down and rushed in without a word to the cabby.

No pains or cost had been spared by its backers to make this newest of Goldfield's hostelries lavish beyond any hope of comparison. All its appointments were the richest to be found, its lobby finished in solid mahogany and furnished with overstuffed leather lounge chairs. Even its pillars were surrounded by oval padded leather seats built against them. There were lounges, too, on both the first and second floors. Half the rooms had private baths and every room was the last word in comfort and luxury — velvet hangings, deep piled carpets, the finest linens and most expensive furniture obtainable. It was a sultan's dream.

Slim was halfway across the palatial lobby before his mind — breaking loose of its conflicts — really saw the crowd or caught up with the silence which, neck deep appeared suddenly to be pressing in all around him like the reach of hooked fingers. Stopped in midstride, confused, head flung up, nose nervously twitching, the avid expectancy — coiled like a snake and foxed with danger — caught him hard by the throat.

His feverish stare picked out Ole Elliott, L. L. Patrick and, off in a corner standing cheek by jowl, Diamondfield Jack Davis, C. D. Taylor, Carltenmore and Governor John Sparks. There were other nabobs sprinkled through the crush. Every newshound in town was there and every eye, by the look, was fixed spang on Slim.

He backed off a step and then, prodded anew by the rage and frustrations churning inside him, too quivering with hate and fired up to be careful, balling both fists and lowering his head he looked about to take off in a wild rush at Ezra.

Before he could do it a hand tugged his sleeve, tugged again with more urgency. An E-string voice complained, "Mister, afore you git kilt I got a fare t' collect."

Somebody sniggered. Other voices broke through and, like a gasp of relief, laughter ran round the walls. Jenkens, wheeling with a curse, found the cabby staring up at him. In a pet Slim flung out the last of his gold pieces. But when he turned back the reporters had closed in, the big name correspondents of the great Eastern dailies.

"Is it true you've gone broke?"

"What's the name of your mine, Slim?"

"What're you going to do about that ore they've impounded?"

"You got any line on that jasper that slugged you?"

"Carltenmore says you've brought in your last sack —"

"Yeah," Slim snarled, "that whey-bellied polecat thinks he's got this whole camp by the seat of the pants! Him an' his Injuns an' gun-wavin' killers! He's cost me with his tricks near half a million dollars but he ain't got the guts to put his pile where his mouth is!"

The uproar had assumed fairly hectic proportions, yet it was evident Carltenmore had got the gist of these remarks. He was waddling forward, triple chins shaking like the jowls of a hog, three of the reporters shoving back to give him room.

"Jenkens," he wheezed with his eyes pretty near popping out of that livid face, "I've stood enough of your nonsense — enough, do you hear? Now hear this, you people — I'm calling his bluff! I'm betting five hundred thousand, against this new mine, he can't fetch another bag of that same kind of ore into this town inside of a week!" A bright shine of triumph glittered back of his stare, as turning to Jenkens, he said, "Put up or shut up."

XVII

Featherstone, nudging Slim, said in a loud whisper, "You're not going to let him get away with that, are you?"

The question, of course, though packed with significance, was largely rhetorical. Wriggle and squirm as Jenkens might he had no choice; he had already lost too much face to back off. The rigged deal was Ezra's specialty and this one — baited with the press and garnished by the presence of such a galaxy of prominent persons — had been meticulously hand-tailored toward the one end result of putting the Death Valley Midas precisely where his arch enemy wanted him. He had to pick up the gauntlet or be laughed out of town.

It was that simple, that cunning, that insufferably evident. The picture roared through Slim's head with the cacophony of catastrophe. Without a string of stashed horses there was no possibility of him reaching his ranch and getting back inside the time limit. Ezra P., once again, was well on his way toward the top of the heap.

Slim had set out to sell the man's greed a

bill of goods and had, ironically, so con-spicuously succeeded that now he stood a mighty good chance to die of it. Despite the assayers and veteran experts like Meyers, regardless of what his *busca* scouts may have told him, Carltenmore's avarice had tipped the scales and he was thor-oughly determined, by fair means or foul, to lay bare the secret of Slim's mysterious horde.

Slim saw the trap, but there was no way around it. Carltenmore wanted him out in the desert where, rushed and harassed by that impossible time limit Slim, to have even the ghost of a chance, must go straight to his source — with Hell Creek and all them damn Injuns hard after him!

Through a red fog of rage, he yelled, "I'll take that! Now dash back to the Mammoth an' redouble yer guards! Git the word to your trackers an' that exterminator, Charlie — put 'em all on my trail. But when I come back have that half million ready! By grab, you'll eat crow if it's the last thing you do!"

And, turning round, he stomped out.

There was no time to waste.

But Jenkens knew, deep inside, he was hamstrung already. Those fine brave words were silly whistles against the dark. He hadn't the chance of a snowball in hell! Given double the time he couldn't have done it. The King's rigged deal was even better than he knew. The ore Old Itchy Paws had just had impounded was the last of the lot — he'd scraped the bottom of the bin. There wasn't enough good rock left out in Death Valley to chink the ribs of a sand flea and the whole dang push was mighty soon going to know it.

With his luck running high and hot enough a man just might, in the time allowed, put together a sack that would hoax Ezra P, but it would never fool those who'd be called to pass judgement. Slim's rock had been a distinctive kind, its peculiar properties fairly well established. It had come from a trove of highgrade he'd turned up in the cinder hills of Ubehebe Crater some four months better than a full year ago, jewelry rock so rotten with gold he'd suspected straight off it had been lifted from the Mammoth; it had the same characteristics as the ore discovered in Slim's original strike, the prospect Carltenmore had hornswoggled him out of.

Biding his time Slim had packed the rock home, playing with it, fondling it, gloating, grading, sacking it, seeing in its astonishing richness a skewer on which he might impale the man who had ruined his life. But in his hate, his cocksureness, he had sold Ezra short, underestimating the man, his boldness and cunning; and now the bright bubble had burst in his face.

Still scanning his chances Slim came into the street. His bitter cerebrations could not find a gleam of hope. That mountain of flesh — that hogfat finagler, had got the best of him again; and *this* time Ezra had really pinned his ears back. Slim might find other ore but it wouldn't get the job done. There was probably, scattered around this town, enough Mammoth highgrade to bring him in a winner; there were a dozen crooked assayers a man might approach if he had anything to deal with. The very notion made Slim groan. He didn't even have a *pot*.

Carltenmore had taken care of that when he'd had Slim robbed and then, to make sure double certain, by a slippery court order had grabbed all his ore. He was whipsawed anyway, chained to the nubbin by the searchlight glare of all those write-ups and notoriety. No cagey fence would dare to deal with him now. There'd be too much heat. He was marked for the slaughter.

167

"Señor — Señor Sleem . . ." A timid hand touched his arm; and Slim found himself staring at Dolores Ramirez in her cheap peasant's dress that, through too many scrubbings, hugged her contours like skin.

He drew back with a curse. It was the final straw, the ultimate ignominy, the awfullest reality of all the miserable thumps fate had slipped him that this — this female, now that he was flat up against it, should come like a fish-tailed Harpy and drag him away to an end worse than death.

"What *is* it?" she whispered, with her round frightened eyes peering into his face. "You're pale as a ghost. Are you sick?" she cried in Spanish.

Her obvious concern appeared to worsen his condition. A kind of shudder writhed through him and, twisting his head, he swiveled a desperate backward look over his shoulder.

"Oho!" the girl said; and then, more complacent, "It is the Carltenmore — no?" and she bobbed her chin, causing the comb standing high in her hair to flash tiny prisms of light through her shawl. An odd little smile ran across the red lips. She looked swiftly about. "Come." She tightened her grip, suddenly tugging him, urgent. "I think no one sees us. We must go from here quickly."

And, before he quite understood what was happening, he was in a carriage with her, speeding away, careening around buildings in the scream of dry wheel hubs, flying wisps of the girl's ink-black hair in his face.

He did not honestly find this unpleasant, or the way she was sometimes thrown hard against him as the lurching vehicle was dragged through potholes and whisked around corners in a clatter of hoofs by their whip-cracking driver. Then the road straightened out, the feel of her moved a little primly away and Jenkens, released from that fragrant, tumultuous — if somewhat grudging — contact, thrust his head from the door and yelled to the driver to stop.

Dolores said with authority, "You have not enough time to do this thing and get back."

Slim, about to step out, paused to peer at her, scowling. "Well," he said, reddening, "I'm not goin' to *your* place."

Her eyes looked back at him. "If it is because of my brother I think you should know my father became very angry at what Tomas did. He has disowned him and sent him away."

When Jenkens had nothing to say about that her eyes dropped to the hands that were clenched in her lap. He looked for tears and entreatments, but this girl had her pride, and she was not beaten yet.

With a toss of her chin she shook the shawl from her cheeks. "I heard what he said — the *patrón*," she informed him, "and your own windy boast. So go! Let them laugh, if that is what you want; but do not take me for a fool, *señor*. You have no mine!"

Something gave a great lurch inside of Slim like scaffolds falling. His mouth sprang open. She didn't wait for his bluster. "All that gold of the stories — all this ore you brought, I think, was his already. You said it was stolen but he could not believe you; do you hope to go back now and take out some more?"

She had some right to the scorn her eyes showed, for this was the crux of it. The only chance he could see for beating Ezra again was to get into the Mammoth, and it couldn't be done — not in the face of all those gun-packing guards.

While he crouched there silent she bade the driver to go on, and the next time he stopped they were in front of Elfego's. She didn't wait to be helped; she was quite strong enough to get down by herself. It came over Slim then in a surge of revulsion she was the strongest dang female he had ever bumped into.

Snarling with disgust he climbed out himself. He'd sustained some hard knocks but not until he'd reached to find a coin for the cabby, and a search of his pockets turned up never a penny, did the cup of his bitterness truly run over.

Dolores paid the man, and he was finally gone, while Slim stood glowering. Trying to salve the delicate matter of his pride the girl tactfully examining the street in both directions, moved onto the stoop and twisted an arrangement that set up a clatter somewhere inside. "My father will be happy you have been concerned for his health."

Jenkens glared but kept his mouth shut. The smallest Ramirez opened the door. Dolores, stepping back, said, "You remember Alfredo?" The boy grinned shyly and Jenkens, grunting, went into the house like a spooky bronc.

He had his own notions about what was up, and they were rudely confirmed when she said to the boy, "The gentleman has come to speak with our father. Will you see that he finds him while I fetch the little cakes?"

The old man seemed weaker but he managed to hoist himself onto his feet long enough to give Slim a tearful *embrazo*. "*Su servidor, señor!* Welcome to my poor house," he said shakily. "It is not often friends come to see Elfego these days," and he sagged back in his chair as though the end was not far.

Jenkens, fiddling with the fine hat he had bought, was too uncomfortable to dig up any small talk, though he did find the grace to ask about the old man's prospects. Elfego wearily shrugged. "For myself it makes no difference. For Dolores, for the *niño,* I have a great sadness. The world you and I know, *señor,* has little kindness. The girl will find a man but, unless he is *simpatico,* who will care for the little one, eh?

"But enough of my troubles. Fortune smiles on you, I think. The papers say —"

Dolores came in just then with the refreshments. "Last night he was robbed of many thousand of pesos which he got for the shares the *pícaro;* Sam Reilly —"

"It don't matter." Slim growled, "I don't care about that."

"And this morning," Dolores said, "the *policía* took away from him the two muleloads of ore he had put in the hotel *caja de caudales.*" And she passed Slim the cakes, put into his hand a blue glass of wine. "You behold a ruined *hombre,* papá."

Elfego looked pained. He wrung his hands in an access of anguish. "Who would do this thing!" he cried, cheeks contorted with an indignation almost as great as if he'd personally been the victim. And Dolores turned with curling lip. "Who, indeed, but the *patrón* —"

"*El Puerco Grande?*"

"The same," she said, and told of what had taken place between the king and Jenkens in the hotel lobby. And, as she spoke, his wrinkled cheeks grew dark until Jenkens, sipping his wine from the hand-crafted blue glass, looked for the old man to have a stroke. But when she told of the climax, of Carltenmore hurling forth his half-a-million-dollar challenge, Elfego wrathfully leaped to his feet in an outburst of Spanish too fierce and fast for Slim's understanding.

Yes, the girl said, Don Enriqué had accepted. What else could he do with so many *gato gordos* looking on? But the terms were impossible. Now he must lose even the source of his wealth, the hidden mine El Puerco's scouts had been trying to wrest from him. "A-a-ai-hé! Such a sadness!" she said; and Elfego clapped his head in despair.

Jenkens helped himself to some more of the grape, having reached in his reflections that fragile perch between the gnashing of teeth and a cloddish acceptance where the most of us after a whaling wind up. Not quite numb, yet fed to the gills with the subject of Ezra and all his damned works, he had shut his ears to this gabble of tongues. But some part of his awareness caught hold of him suddenly, knifed by the flash of his host's dark stare.

"I think a small sack would do it," Dolores was saying, "if the quality stands up." And now they were eying each other like eagles.

Jenkens' heart gave a lurch. The old man nodded and the girl, jumping up, kicked off her *guarachas* and ran from the room. Slim had only the vaguest of inklings, but excitement and danger were in the air like a smell.

Dolores came back, breathing hard, eyes burning like stars as she dropped two heavy chunks of rock in his lap. He carried them over to the window with a roaring in his head, hands shaking as he turned them about in the light. He stared across the room at the grinning Elfego. "This looks pretty fair. You got any more of it?"

"Poco más."

Slim studied it again, rubbing it against the sole of his boot, scratching it with the sight of his pistol. Scowling fiercely he hammered a piece with the butt, and there was no doubt about it. This was Mammoth ore of extremely high quality.

He drew a long breath. "Got enough fer one sack?"

The old man nodded.

With half a million dollars at stake, not to mention such sundries as revenge and lost face, Slim reckoned a man had ought to be pretty careful. He had other thoughts, too, stepping around Dolores to put the rocks on the table. He stared again at Elfego, wondering if it was the wine that made this deal trot so slick. "What do you want?" he said to him finally, and some of the suspicion got into his voice.

The old man looked surprised, sort of hurt and someway baffled and, in his perplexity, turned to peer at the girl.

She said, "The Yanquis do not give things away without expectation of something in return. He wants to know what you're after, what you think to get back in exchange for the gold that will turn away laughter and make him the *rico* he wants so desperately to be."

Jenkens, ignoring the girl and her scorn,

tipped the nod to her father. "That's it," he said gruffly. "How much'll it come to?"

"No, no!" Elfego protested, vigorously shaking his head.

"I do this for you, *señor*. Because we are *amigos*. Well — maybe just a little for the *despecho* — for spite," he grinned. "But for a profit — no! Take it and welcome. Let us only hope it will make that pig squirm!"

XVIII

The hour was late in a night turned the color of ink dropped in water when Slim with his two hulking mules came into the Bullfrog Hills above Rhyolite. The crags of two great peaks stood stark against the heavens, offering compass readings he wouldn't normally have noticed. But nothing about this trek was ordinary — least of all the continued bleak prowl of Slim's termagant thoughts.

These, ever and furious, doubt-ridden, intolerable, kept fresh in his mind the parting looks of that girl. Never in his life had he felt so unsettled, so jumpy and dubious, so filled with forebodings or racked with suspicions. That sack of Mammoth highgrade Dolores had put together with Elfego's blessing should have made his prospects right again, bright with promise; and it had — for the moment. Yet even while Alfredo was fetching the mules a chill had come over Slim that now was crawled deep into his bones. No matter what that old coot had crazily said, nothing worth having was like to drop in your lap.

There was a price tag on everything; and he was just about convinced he'd traded the rest of his tomorrows — probably mortgaged himself straight into double harness, for that miserable sack of stolen yellow rock. It was in the memory of her eyes, that sly and twisted little smile as, hands on hips, she had watched him go.

He had left himself one chance to squeeze free by not taking the ore, ordering it held in readiness against his return. This caginess, however, had served only to muddle without by one hair improving his outlook. He knew goddamn well he'd go back if he was able!

He slunk past the Rhyolite road without stopping, cursing his mules to the south and west in the direction of Leadville and Titus Canyon to throw off, if he could any redskins Charlie might have cruising these knobs. Still short of the canyon road he cut east to bypass Thimble Peak which he could see in the distance as night's dark lost its grip on the hours. In a clump of brush he paused for a bit to blow the mules while considering his chances of slipping past Ezra's cordon of watchdogs.

The most of them had probably been pretty close in but Charlie's scouts with their breech-loading rifles would be stashed all over, belly-down in the rim-rocks, hungrily waiting to pick up his sign. So far as that went he *wanted* them to see him — it was what he'd come out for, to make them and Hell Creek look a pack of damn fools. And maybe give those reporters something to write about. He didn't expect Charlie's Injuns to burn up much powder, not until anyways they'd got a line on his mine — which he reckoned it would be a little hard for them to do. But the more of these miles he could put behind in darkness the less of Ezra's understrappers he was going to have to contend with; and a few of them sports like that dude of a Titus, and maybe one or two of them grudge-packing shopkeepers, might not be above trying to drop him if they could line their sights where there wasn't no witnesses.

He struck out for the buttes above Stovepipe Wells. The sun came up and got hot on his back and the mules grew increasingly hard to control. Occasionally he had to use some pretty stiff language, but along about noon the buttes began to show up against the rimming mountains, the barbaric colors of the naked rock shimmering in the heat curling off the valley floor.

The striped and folded red-and-black flanks of the Grapevines now were a good piece behind and Slim's eyes, backward pulled across the twist of one shoulder, held of a sudden the hard sheen of agate. A thin column of smoke was standing high in the blue above Corkscrew Peak; and, even as he watched, it broke into a series of signal-like puffs.

He threw a leg over Zachary Taylor's flattening ears and, sliding off, pulled all his gear, transferring it to Gretchen. She heaved up a disgusted snort. And when he hoisted a boot to yank the slack from the trunk strap she displayed her ill humor by attempting to sink her teeth in the seat of the gorgeous striped pants Petz had cut out and sewed for him.

"You want a hump in yer nose?" Jenkens snarled, jumping back. "By grab, you keep on you'll sure as hell git one!"

He knocked the wind from her belly, jerked the cinch tighter and, anchoring the strap with a four-in-hand knot, swung aboard and gave her a taste of the steel. She hid her spleen a little better after that — for a while. Then Zach took a notion to play with his halter rope. Slim put a boot under his chin to discourage this, and the loco old fool began dragging his feet. Slim unsnapped the rope and the mule, cocking his ears, obnoxiously heehawed, silly as an ass until Jenkens, scowling, shook out the rope's end. With a loud blat the old fraud took to his heels.

A couple hours later, crossing Mesquite Flat, Slim saw a smoke spiraling over Tucki Mountain. Before they'd gone another mile several puffs climbed through the snags of the Panamints. Jenkens grinned. Charlie's Shoshonies had him spotted.

If he had been trying to hide he could have gone straight ahead, getting into the cover of piñon and juniper. Instead he cut south, heading into the sand dunes, hoping this could fetch them hard on his trail. He had no mind to be wearing himself to a frazzle while Hell Creek and his scouts sat around in the pines smoking and laughing, comfortably laved by cool breezes.

He was traveling light, spreading his own weight over both mules, riding relay, with just enough grub for one more meal. And, by the growls gurgling through him, it was sure about due. In the gunnysack back of his saddle he had about one good feed for the mules. Beyond this, and the weight of his rifle, the only other thing he had bothered to fetch was a short-handled shovel.

In the short four hours still left before dark there were a number of things he had to get done if he was minded to pull Ezra's spies out of the rimrocks.

He could, if he chose, bend more to the east and still forge south at the edge of the salt marshes below the rose-and-umber wrinkles of Tucki Mountain. He could plow through the arrowweed of the Devil's Cornfield, which he'd sure have to do if he went that way.

These dunes, with their loose yellow sand, spread over considerable ground and had already been flagged when, with Flinch Eye's help, he'd been setting this up. He had a cache eight miles east of Koger Mountain, a cache in Racetrack Alley, one in the bubbles of Emigrant Wash, one just north of the abandoned stone walls of Panamint City, still another in the barren yellow-browns of Panamint Valley, and a last one close by the site of Skidoo. But these, he thought now, had better be forgotten, at least for the moment. If his luck in these sand hills didn't hold up, he might have to run for it in sure-enough earnest; but if things got that bad he'd be whipped anyway, unable to make Goldfield inside the King's deadline. Meanwhile, he reckoned, these dunes would do nicely. Twenty-five square miles should be enough room for anyone.

There was only one drawback: if the wind got up bad a man could leave his bones in this place. Sometimes, during a gale, the sand would rise in a great swirling mass and pretty near fill the whole trough of Death Valley with a gritty yellow fog through which nothing could be seen — not even the goddamn sun! But it had been pretty quiet when he'd come through with the Paiute and it had in Slim's opinion, one paramount advantage. It was about as dry as a country could get. There wasn't one spring in the whole length and breadth of it. If Carltenmore's understrappers chased him in here they would dang quick wish they'd never heard of his mine. Their tongues would be out a foot and forty inches before they'd covered the first ten miles!

He climbed one of the sculptured dunes and, shading his eyes, picked out Tucki Mountain. You'd of thought, with all that smoke, you was staring at Vesuvius about to kick off. Them scouts sure were busy.

Floundering back to firmer ground among the mesquites, creosote and four-winged saltbush, he considered the lacework of trails made by small rodents zigzagging across the sand. In a matter of hours the hoofs of horses would be sinking new paths across this waste, tracks which might last for as long as six months or be filled by a shift of the wind in six minutes.

He considered the mules and decided, after slanching a glance at the sun, he might as well feed them here as some other place. They could do with a rest and, that way — if he had to — he could make a bigger jump before blowing them again. The nearest tin can spring was a good many whoops and hollers farther west and he would just as lief cover the largest part of it after dark. Hell, he might as well make them buggers earn their stipends.

He pulled his hull and spread the blanket hair-side up to get the sweat dried out of it after first making sure the local mesquites were bare of beans; this was no dang time to be immobilized with bloat. While the mules were grinding up the last of the grain he worked through a couple of mouthfuls of jerky, stomping around to get the give back into his saddle-cramped legs, keeping well away from the sparse shade of bushes. He wasn't scared of snakes. He wasn't in the mood to curl up with one, neither.

When he thought they were cool enough

he sparingly watered Gretchen and Zach, wet down his own throat, shook the bag to see how much there was left and wondered if he dared leave the thing to goad Charlie. If Ezra's man Friday latched onto the notion his quarry had somehow run short of water it just might spur him to some unconsidered action. Like sticking too close to Slim's heels to turn loose.

It was worth a try, anyway. Slim knew where he could get more; he did not think it likely the king's exterminator would. If a man could run that bunch out of water. . . .

His eyes began to glint as they prowled the deep hush. Sand and heat and the solemn quiet of this brooding desolation could be terrible things — deciding factors, if a man used them right. Catching up blanket and saddle, darkly pondering, he approached Zachary Taylor.

The mule's ears came up. He softly blew through his nose and began to back off. Jenkens, swearing, made a lunge for the critter. That was all Zach needed. With a frightened snort he took off like a jack rabbit.

Slim, glowering, stood stunned, then broke into a run. But he soon had to quit. The sand was too heavy for that kind of travel, the air too damned hot. Zach was gone like a twister, hellbent for the back-trail. Slim was too beat to curse.

Panting, the sweat cracking through his pores like rain, he floundered back to where Gretchen was pruning new growth from the mesquites. He grabbed a handful of halter and bulldogged her over to where he'd dropped his gear.

Time he got her ready he figured there wasn't one bit of moisture left in him, so he had himself another pull from the waterbag. Pouring the rest of it into his chin-strapped straw, he held it till she'd sucked up the last drop. He put the hat on then and pitched the water sack away.

This, and the tracks, made a pretty convincing picture, he thought, of a man turned desperate. And a twisted grin briefly touched his lean mouth. Maybe it was a good thing he'd lost Zach at that. They were bound to think now he would head for his mine by the shortest route. If anything would pull Charlie out of the rimrocks and glue him to whatever tracks Slim might leave, this ought to.

But Zachary Taylor's defection had played serious havoc with Jenkens' mobility and cut his edge of Hell Creek almighty thin. He still had the advantage of knowing this country as well if not better than Charlie's Shoshonies, but he no longer had that safe margin of speed. They could move — for a while — about as quickly as he could. And, if Charlie used what brains God had given him, they might even manage to get near enough for gunplay. When a man has a specialty, he likes to show it off. Jenkens had no doubt that son of a bitch would shoot if he ever got close enough, and he would sure as hell try if he latched onto the notion Slim was running him around through this sand just for kicks.

Slim wasn't — not really, but it might seem so to Hell Creek if it finally became apparent Slim wasn't going to even go *near* any mine.

He did everything he could with his tracks to slow them down. Without Zach to fall back on he was forced to pamper Gretchen a deal more than he liked. He rested her frequent, not pushing her now, trying to hold some of her strength in reserve. Mules generally, in his experience, were more rugged than horses, and most times Slim took advantage of the fact. He dared not now. If they ever put him afoot he was done. And he knew it.

Nor were these the only handicaps Zach's departure had hung round Slim's neck. He had to give the appearance of a man trying hard to hang onto his lead, a man determined to reach and get away from his mine not only before they could catch a good look at him, but in such a way as would keep them from finding it. Since the mine was fictitious this might take some doing.

He couldn't even be sure he'd pulled them after him, though this had to be his assumption. He could not afford to have them watching and pondering every move he made. He had to have them hard after him with no time for cool judgements; and when their water ran low, as it must in good season, they had to seem near enough to replenish where he did.

This was the essence of Slim's entire strategy, only now it must be managed with four legs instead of eight. Mule legs, unpredictable; and if they couldn't cut it he stood to lose half a million, very possibly even his life. What had started as a laugh on Ezra had now turned dangerously serious — about as deadly a game as a man could play.

One hour past dark under a sky filled

with stars Slim was in the vicinity of his nearest flagged cache, the buried food and precious water, all he would have to go on until well into the following morning — and he could not find the flag.

He divided the area into circles and angles, crisscrossed them, not once but a dozen times, but the flag he'd put up — a piece of old shirttail — had completely disappeared. He thought at first it had blown over, but it simply wasn't there. He was so certain this was the correct location he even fetched his shovel and gophered around for pretty near half an hour before, reminded of passing time by Gretchen's impatient stomping, he finally gave up and climbed back in the saddle. The only answer he could hit on was wind had shifted some of these dunes, maybe built a new hill where he'd buried his cans.

He swung the mule south two miles by guess, then pointed her east in a poor frame of mind. It was an unsettling business, but at least he was lucky it had happened at night. With the sun beating down they'd have been in bad straits. By pushing Gretchen a little while it was relatively cool he hoped to make up enough lost time to reach his next cache before, if possible, the sun got up. What he had in mind was a good rest for both of them.

He kept his eyes peeled. Darkness wouldn't slow Charlie down much. Those Injuns could pretty near track a wood tick across solid rock, and desert country at night never did get as dark as most other places. In spite of attempts to conceal it he reckoned the most of his sign was plain as plowed ground.

He didn't make many rest stops but he watched Gretchen close to be sure he wasn't giving her more than she could take. The place he was bound for was the best of the lot if he was put in the position of having to defend it. A low rock hill cropping out of the sand, it was the only location he hadn't bothered to flag. Without it was buried by a shift of the dunes there was no chance he'd miss it with its top towering over the sands like a butte. He'd been past that cairn half a hundred times going to and from town without guessing till he'd climbed it what a hideout the place could be. It's top was a twenty-foot craterlike depression holding ample space to conceal a dozen horses. Its eastern slope was a tangle of piñon and juniper, nothing but sand and rocks covering the rest of it. And it was high enough to be seen for a good piece.

In the shank of the night Slim began to

watch for it. He was pretty near pooped and the mule didn't look to be in much better shape. They were going to have to stop soon, regardless. Twice in the past half hour he'd jerked out of a doze to find Gretchen all but stopped in her tracks. The most he could get out of her now was a walk. He tried walking himself to save all he could of her; and an hour short of dawn he saw the knob he was hunting.

It was still the best part of a couple miles off.

It occurred to him as they went wallowing toward it that without Zach in tow he'd better figure an extra day to getting back, maybe more if Charlie's bunch gave much of a chase.

Now and again he peered over his shoulder, not really expecting to see Charlie but increasingly nervous, filled with some nameless foreboding. Something seemed to be trying to call itself to his attention. He stared hard at the rocks, he even watched Gretchen's ears, but if danger was stalking them she remained unaware of it.

He guessed the whole thing probably stemmed from his condition; he felt, by grab, like he'd been hauled through a knothole. Every joint of him ached, every muscle felt jumpy. He stopped Gretchen to listen, getting down on his knees to put an ear to the ground. The desert's vast hush lay unbroken around him.

There just wasn't anything to hear, he told himself, trying to scoff away this tension. He went on; Gretchen, grunting, breaking into motion back of him. It was a kind of minor agony just to pick up his feet any more, but he kept doing it, doggedly whittling down the footage still interposed between himself and the cairn.

Now the rock showed plainly, and he began to think about that can of buried water, hurrying a little, pulling away from the mule. He was halfway up the scabrous slope when the whang of a gun locked him stiff in his tracks.

XIX

A scream tore through the reverberations of the report. A naked shape lurched upright on the rim of the butte, abruptly plunging from sight. Jenkens, coming out of his trance, remembered his rifle and looked for the mule. She was standing, indifferent, at the base of the slope.

Somewhere above there was a further commotion, something moving through shale. Slim grabbed out his pistol. A horse nickered faintly as he went clambering upward in short zigzag dashes, low crouched, almost gasping, ready to fire if anyone appeared. While he was still a dozen feet from the rim something waved in the grayness back of where the gone shape had showed. Mightily tempted, Slim held his fire. "Show yerself," he wheezed through his panting. "Git up where I can git a good look at you!"

For an eternity nothing happened. No sound could be heard but his own labored gasps. The band of gray opening up between fade of stars and the more distinct, harsher cleavage of reality was widening, lightening, appearing less like fog, when a guttural voice somewhere above gruffly bade, "You come. All safe now."

Tugged between the clutch of anger and the shakes sprung from relief and feeling about as foolish as a twenty-two cartridge in an eight-gauge gun, the Midas of Death Valley came slowly, glowering, to his feet. "Dad grab you, Flinch Eye! What's the matter with you? Don't you know I mighta filled you full of more danged holes than a bakin' soda lid!"

He was sure-enough riled.

"Me shootum!" the Paiute said, proud as Punch.

"How'd that bugger git up there?"

"Me chasum!"

Slim got his legs to working again. "Thought I told you to stay at the ranch —"

"Alla time me stay!" Flinch Eye yelled like he was affronted. That was the trouble with these Injuns. They was no more responsible than a tankful of sheep dip. Put a gun in their fists, all they could think of was killing!

Slim whistled up Gretchen, then climbed into the depression and dug up his cans while the Paiute set about building a fire. Slim poured his hat full of oats from the grub can, loosened the chin strap and

194

flopped it over the mule's eager ears. He was looking for a stick he could skewer the bacon onto when he happened to catch a good look at the fire. With a curse, fighting mad, he yanked Gretchen's blanket away from the Injun. "What the hell're you up to?"

"Make talk." Flinch Eye scowled. "Smoke say 'Go home — him dead!' "

"Great," Jenkens said, too dog-tired to argue. "All right, you made it." He pitched the blanket aside. "No more smoke!" He kicked apart the Paiute's fire, stamping out everything but a few glowing coals. Over these he fixed his bacon, dividing it with Flinch Eye, then hacked open the two tins of peaches he'd pawed out of Gretchen's oats. When there was nothing left to eat he slipped back to the rim and had a look through his glass. He gave it five minutes without spotting a thing. But he was a long way from satisfied.

Been about as hard as pulling teeth, but while they'd been eating he'd got a few facts from Flinch Eye. Two days ago Charlie had showed up at the ranch with the pick of his scouts, half a dozen it seemed. They had caught Flinch Eye napping and had ransacked the place; had worked Flinch Eye over and left him for dead. Came out from their talk they'd found two of Slim's camps. When the Paiute was able he'd looked for their sign, dogged the one set of tracks which had wound up right here. Then he'd hunkered down to wait. When the Shoshoni had peered through his sights to pot Slim the Paiute had let him have it.

It didn't look good any way you sized it up. Jenkens reckoned the sooner he struck out for Goldfield the longer he'd have to catch the ear of the Lord. But he couldn't go yet. First he had to rest Gretchen. He fell asleep thinking about it.

It was about three by the sun when Flinch Eye roughly shook him awake. He had Slim's glass in his hand and appeared excited. "You look!" he grunted, pointing west with a swing of his loud-smelling arm.

Slim grabbed the glass and slithered up to where he could peer between rocks. A jag of horsebackers showed against the sand. It was them, all right! He could see the flash of rifle barrels and the sun bearing down on naked shoulders, and the one in the lead had on a black hat.

Nobody had to tell Slim it was Hell Creek. The whole bunch was bound arrow-straight for this butte. They were about three miles off, not using whips but not getting off, neither, to hunt for no posies.

Slim scrambled back to the Paiute. "Here! Pour some of that agua into my bonnet, git yourself a drink an' pitch the rest away."

He took the hat slopping over to Gretchen, let her wet her gums, then sloshed the rest of it over himself. After which, retrieving his rifle but paying no mind to blanket or saddle, he caught up her halter shank and hustled her down through the brush growing out of the east slope, into which the Paiute had already vanished.

By keeping that knob of tumbled rocks between themselves and Ezra's oncoming outfit Slim hoped to stretch their lead a good five or six miles before they were spotted, but it soon became evident this was wasted wishing. They had hardly gone more than two miles from their water stop when Flinch Eye, excitedly brandishing his rifle, growled, "Pretty soon come!"

Slim, twisting for a look, had to peer through his glass before he could bring the view close enough to pick out the motionless figure at the top of a dune. Even as he looked the Shoshoni whirled his calico pony and dissolved from sight in a flutter of dust. Flinch Eye grinned. "Not come yet. First git drink!" And he showed his bad teeth in an audible chuckle.

Slim laughed, too, at the picture of Charlie coming onto those cans. But he sobered uncomfortably, knowing from repute the man's probable reaction when he saw the scattered grain they had decided to abandon, Slim's saddle and blanket and the wet place where they'd dumped the last of the water. The King's pet hatchet man would go hog wild!

This, of course, was what Slim had geared this whole trek to, but it looked a lot different out here than when he'd planned it. Charlie had no choice. If he was to come up with Slim at all he'd have to do it right quick; and it was mighty soon apparent he meant to throw everything he had into the try.

Before Slim had covered another half mile the whole bunch were in sight, coming like hell emigrating on cart wheels. "Me shootum!" Flinch Eye grinned, preparing to drop out of leather.

"You stay on that horse an' keep whackin'!"

The Paiute hissed like a coiling rattler, half lifting his rifle, but Slim's look never wavered. Neither did Flinch Eye's craving to count coup. The next time he tried to get off to test his eyesight Slim's yell was late. The Paiute lit rolling, the rifle kicking in his hands while Slim was trying to get stopped. Slim had reckoned the distance too great for a hit, but two shapes swayed, and one went off the back of his horse. The second, humped over the saddle, pulled up. Then a horse went down and the rest swung wide, two of them wheeling back toward the stopped one. But the black hat of Charlie never swerved by an inch.

Slim yelled at Flinch Eye, reaching down to give him a hand. Bent over the rifle, trying to get it reloaded, the Paiute didn't even so much as look up. After that he couldn't have got up if he'd wanted to. One of Charlie's slugs caught him square in the brisket. Slim whirled the mule and got out of there fast.

The rested Gretchen, watered and fed, was in a lot better shape than Charlie's gasping hard-pushed horse. He came on for a while. The next time Slim looked there was pretty near a mile between him and Charlie, and the game but ruined horse appeared about due to fold. The last Slim saw of Carltenmore's killer there wasn't anything under him but the burn of yellow sand.

At the hotel bar the crowd was five deep and the odds against Jenkens, as currently posted, stood at sixty to one with but a half hour to go. The extravagant splendor of the lobby, ablaze with lights, was a confluence of the mighty. All the Goldfield notables appeared to be on tap; and sandwiched in along the fringes were others — like Elfego — who were remarkable mainly for the strangeness of their presence. It was a boisterous affair and about the largest turnout the town, prior to the Gans-Nelson extravaganza, ever had assembled. Consensus of opinion was that the Death Valley Midas — his bluff shrewdly called by that best of good fellows, their host, E. P. Carltenmore — had packed up his tent and done a bolt for greener pastures.

The minutes crept inexorably by. The babble of voices became more exuberant. The odds favoring Ezra leaped like a mountain goat. It was a hilarious gathering, a night to date time from.

By the King's watch there was scarcely ten minutes to go and, with that mine on his mind, he wasn't sure whether he should chuckle or snarl when Slim, on Gretchen, rode in through the door.

He was dusty, unshaven, with a hard

tight look in the corners of his eyes that perhaps were remembering his last glimpse of Charlie trying to walk himself out of the squish of that sand. Then he pulled back his head, that bright stare passing Featherstone to fasten on Ezra where he stood with Pheppy Titus. He shoved a sack off his lap that hit the floor with a clunk.

The king's face went pale as Titus and Blackey Dawson taking nothing for granted, hurried forward to cut it open. Alva Myers and George Nixon were in the forefront of those who avidly closed in, and just behind them was Tex Rickard, a gambler's smile spread across his lips. Necks craned through the coffin-like silence as the sack was cut open right there on the floor. Carltenmore's eyes almost popped from his head as the chunks were dumped out. The crowd gasped. Mere words could not do justice to the spectacular quality of the ore. Perhaps Alva D. came closest when he said in almost a whisper, "That bag alone should run twenty-five thousand."

The crowd looked stunned.

Ezra P., sounding strangled, demanded of Dawson, "But is it the *same?*"

"It *looks* the same," Blackey said. "It's damn near pure gold." He shot a glance up at Jenkens, wet his lips and stood up, handing a piece of it to Carltenmore who looked about ready to go into a convulsion.

Jenkens said to the assayer, "Why don't you tell him it come outa the Mammoth? Ain't that what you're paid fer?"

Dawson flushed but kept his temper. "In my opinion, it —"

"Don't be an ass!" Ezra snapped. In the face of Jenkens' grin he made an herculean effort to pull himself together. "All right," he said with what dignity he could, "you have won the wager. You'll get your money."

"Just put it in John Crook's bank for me," said Jenkens. "My head's not as hard as I reckoned it was."

This allusion to the night he'd been struck down at Sullivan's brought a few nervous titters out of some of those present; but Carltenmore, livid, drove straight to his goal. "What'll you take for that mine?" he cried harshly. "Name your price!"

Jenkens shook his head.

But the king was not to be stood off. He had never in his life taken No for an answer, and he plainly wasn't about to begin now. "Put a price on it, man! Anything in reason. Here!" he said, whipping out his notebook and fountain pen. He pushed them at Slim in a lather of impatience. "A gentleman's agreement — these people can bear witness. We'll form a company. For fifty-one per cent, and your location of the mine *on paper*, I'll pay you half a million dollars!"

With a sigh and a shrug Jenkens took Ezra's pen and, balancing the notepad on the slant of one knee, scribbled a few words, tore the sheet loose and passed it, folded, to the king.

The hush was tremendous as the great man, opening it, clipped on his pince-nez. He looked staggered. A terrible groan squeezed between his clenched teeth. His face the color of old cheese he collapsed in his tracks, the paper fluttering from his hand.

Featherstone read aloud from the sheet the description Slim had written of Carltenmore's Mammoth, the mine the king had possessed for a paltry three hundred.

When some of the hubbub eased off a wee fraction, Scoop Featherstone said, "You're a rich man, Slim. What'll you do with all that money?"

"I can't hardly realize —"

"You'll get it," Scoop said. "My readers'll see to that. Guess you'll be living it up like a nabob."

"Don't think so."

"You going back to the hills?"

"Might."

"Well, for Pete's sake," Scoop growled, "give me something I can put in the papers. What about that little Ramirez girl? You going to see more of her?"

Slim got Gretchen turned around, and looked queerly back. "You may have somethin' there," he said, and rode off through the cheers of those who'd cashed in from the King's mighty fall.

We hope you have enjoyed this Large Print book. Other Thorndike, Wheeler or Chivers Press Large Print books are available at your library or directly from the publishers.

For more information about current and upcoming titles, please call or write, without obligation, to:

Publisher
Thorndike Press
295 Kennedy Memorial Drive
Waterville, ME   04901
Tel. (800) 223-1244

Or visit our Web site at:
www.gale.com/thorndike
www.gale.com/wheeler

OR

Chivers Large Print
published by BBC Audiobooks Ltd
St James House, The Square
Lower Bristol Road
Bath BA2 3SB
England
Tel. +44(0) 800 136919
email: bbcaudiobooks@bbc.co.uk
www.bbcaudiobooks.co.uk

All our Large Print titles are designed for easy reading, and all our books are made to last.